DARKNESS RISING

DARKNESS RISING

Dark Days Book One

NORMA HALL

orking out. She is a single mom to three amazing boys, daughter to an endearing father, sister to two awesome siblings and she's the coolest aunt there is.11

I dedicate this book to my wonderful Aunt Norma who inspired me to follow in her writing footsteps, my sister Natasha and best friend Vanessa for encouraging and motivating me to follow my heart, and to all of my family and friends who were there for me through some of the darkest days of my life.

Without your love and support, this book would not be here today. Thank you so much for helping me make this dream come true.
Love you all!

Contents

Prologue

I've been watching her since the day she was born. This is how it's always been for us. Every century since our change, we've watched over the Saga lineage. We made a promise to her, to Selene.

Our curse may have begun to forever punish us for our crimes, but I just as Selene, believed we have a much bigger purpose. We must protect the Saga lineage and the Visceral Stone at all costs.

The Stone has been lost to us for ages. No one knows where it is. The last I laid eyes upon it was during the first war of our kind.

Some believe it was lost in the Teutoburg Forest in the 9th Century and that the Forest engulfed it to protect it from the hands of those who might wield it for their own selfish gains.

Some believe Selene cast one last spell at the moment of her release to keep it hidden, only allowing her lineage the ability to find it.

Though, after all these years and all of the Saga's I've encountered, none have ever felt its power call to them, and none have ever had Selene's abilities.

Selene was the most powerful Saga of them all, though the strength of the Vis Selene had inside her was always connected to the Visceral Stone, and only more powerful the closer she was to it. When she gave birth to Senia, her connection to the Stone was finally released and her hold on *The Cursed* was broken.

The Vis was passed down to Senia the moment she was born, though dormant until her 16th birth year. Each Saga that reaches their 16th birth year opens the flood gates to the power of the Vis and must learn to control it before it controls them.

She is already 18 and the Vis is still dormant, something we purposefully wanted in order to keep her hidden from the Council and *The Cursed*. The Council has always manipulated Saga's for their own gain. Genevieve most of all.

Genevieve was used and abused until she lost who she was altogether. No one understood that the Vis takes a toll on the body and that the wielders soul can be overtaken by its dark energy. The Council learned this the hard way with Genevieve when she nearly exterminated us all.

After Genevieve's near obliteration of us, the Council began hunting her Saga lineage and annihilating them before their 16th birth year, hoping to cut off the bloodline so that Vis would die with them.

What the Council didn't know, was that Genevieve had twin daughters. One was taken away at birth and hidden from the Council. Her surviving daughter continued the Saga line with her daughter, and her daughter after that. Therefore, her lineage survived.

For hundreds of years, Genevieve's secret was kept hidden. Until SHE was born... Mia. Her birth lit up a beacon to *The Cursed*. Her energy was felt from all over the world.

There's something about her power and we will all soon learn what it is.

One

I lie awake in bed thinking about my Mom and Dad. It's been three years since they were taken from me. Today would have been my mother's 44th birthday.

I spent a good part of the day thinking about all the times my Dad and I arranged something special for her. My mom wasn't a fan of being the center of attention, but she loved our birthday surprises.

The last birthday celebration Dad and I put together was most special because it was her last. Dad and I decided to surprise Mom with a candlelight dinner for three.

We ran string lights all around the back Pergola and set a small dinner table in the middle. We then set up a small fire pit next to the table to set the ambiance and of course keep us warm. Dad grilled steaks while I made homemade twice baked potatoes and a side salad.

Mom loved it. She didn't care much for gifts, just simple suggestions to show we love her. God how I miss them.

They would be proud of me, thrilled even, that I'm now a Duke Blue Devil. I was fortunate enough to have so many choices but, in the end, Duke was all I wanted, and really needed.

Truthfully, distance is the main reason I'm here. I wanted to be as far away from my past as I could get, like three thousand miles away.

I wanted to try and forget about what happened, find normalcy in my new life. Move on. But nothing happens overnight. It took me months to even open up about what happened... what I saw.

Even still, three years later and I can't forget, I can't move on.

Memories of Mom and Dad always lead me back to the worst memory of all, the reason they're no longer here.

As my mind dwells on the past, tears begin to form as the memory of their murder resurfaces. Going home that night to find their lifeless bodies will forever be engraved in my mind. Lying in misery, my body instantly curls into a ball, trying to withdraw from the suffering that possesses me.

I stare at the clock wondering if I'll ever go to sleep. It's 2:30 a.m. and all I've managed to do is stare into the night letting the tears pool and blur my vision.

As my vision fades, so does the present, and I find myself back in Mandy's room once again.

Three Years Earlier

Mandy goes on and on about dress shopping for our graduation ceremony and her big after party.

Graduation is only two weeks away and she is already on the hunt.

"Ooh I love this dress. This would be perfect for the after party."

I look at the picture Mandy found in the magazine and nearly spit out my gum.

"Good luck wearing something like that. Your mom and your three brothers would totally kill you. The cleavage is so low I can see her belly button."

"I'm 18 now Mia and we graduate in a couple of weeks. My mother has little say in what I get to wear now."

I laugh at Mandy's sudden boldness. She just turned 18 and already thinks she's classified as an adult. "Mandy...you still live with your parents. Enough said."

Mandy turns and looks at me with an evil eye. "Hey...whose side are you on here?"

"You might as well wear pasties and a bandage across your vagina. Or just wear a big flashing sign that says "Slut".

"Wow...why didn't I think of that? How about I just wear body paint?" she says with sly sarcasm.

"Eh hem...Slut." I cough.

Mandy shoves me laughing. "Whatev. I have a nice body. Why not show it off before I get old and have kids that will likely ruin it. So what if I want to look good for all the senior guys I didn't get to screw so they have one lasting impression."

"Wow. That would be you're rational. Apparently, Prom wasn't enough."

Mandy smiles and looks as if she's happily daydreaming. Prom was only a month ago and from the looks of it, the memory of it still beams across her face. She looked amazing that night. Guys were jaw dropped by her scandalous red dress. It was so skin tight there wasn't much left to the imagination but that didn't mean the guys didn't imagine and Mandy loved every minute of it.

"Okay...so I have a game plan. I have six places in mind for us to shop at. We have got to hit the floor running."

Shopping for a Graduation dress is ridiculous since we will be wearing caps and gowns. But...Mandy has a plan for us. Two dresses, one for the ceremony and one for the after party.

I'm so thrilled.

My only problem is that I dread shopping. Anyone who is Mandy's friend would hate shopping since her idea of buying one thing turns into buying a million things and spending hours doing it.

Mandy is blatantly aware of my hatred for shopping, still she makes me suffer her torture; running from store to store and spending an obscene amount of money on something that will shortly after be deemed "last season".

Someone kill me.

Don't get me wrong, I love fashion. I just hate all the work that comes with it.

As she continues to talk about "her" shopping endeavors, my cell rings. It's my mom.

"Hey sweetie...time to come home. Dinner will be ready in twenty minutes."

"Okay...be there soon. I just have to stop by the mailbox on the way home and drop off your letter. I totally forgot this morning. Sorry mom."

"That's okay...as long as you get it in the mailbox. I'll see you soon. Love you!"

"K. Love you too!"

One thing the Williams family members never miss is family dinners. It's the best family pass time. We all have such busy schedules that it's hard to really know what's going on with one another. So...dinner helps fill in the cracks.

I rise from the pile of magazines on Mandy's bed to gather my backpack and car keys.

"I gotta go. Dinner. What time do you want me to pick you up tomorrow?" I ask.

"I have to work in the morning. I get out around noon so pick me up from work would ya?"

"Okay."

Just as I start heading towards the door, I realize what Mandy just said. "Wait. You're going to the mall in your *Chavez Tacos* uniform?"

"NO! Are you serious?!! I'll bring a change of clothes to work with me and just change in your car."

"Well that will fix your look...but what's going to help the chorizo smell?" I say teasingly.

Still totally engulfed by her magazine, Mandy rolls her eyes and shakes her head back and forth mocking me.

I can't help but laugh. "I'll see you tomorrow then. Just please don't keep me at the mall all afternoon. You know I hate being there for hours."

She finally looks up at me with an eyebrow raised. "You sure don't mind it after I make you look like a total hottie do you?"

Uh oh...there goes that Latin spice/sarcasm kicking in. *Such an enormous persona for such a small thing.*

"Yeah...yeah...take it easy there tiger."

Mandy may flaunt a dazzling smile along with her big puppy-dog brown eyes, but she can easily turn into a sassy bitch.

What I love about Mandy is how easily she can be herself. Being as beautiful, stylish and popular as she is, I guess it comes with the territory.

Come to think of it, the majority of my friends are pretty gorgeous. Sometimes I have to crack out the whip to tame the overwhelming beasts from attacking.

How I ended up being a part of the hottie crowd I have no idea. I'm pretty plain Jane compared to the others. I like fashion but I don't obsess about it. Blue jeans and a cute crop top or T suits me just fine. I wear makeup but I don't pack on layers of it because it would take a miracle to hide the freckles on my cheeks. I have long dark brown hair that almost looks black. I'm lean but still shapely, but nothing special. The only thing going for me is my gray eyes. I'm just your average teenage girl.

My popularity compared to my beauty queen friends is a little different too. I openly talk to everyone at school. I don't just stick with my click all day every day.

The beauty queens on the other hand have a reputation to up-hold...so they say. I don't give a rats-ass what people think about me or who I hang with. I usually stay out of all the high school drama.

Well...I almost stay out of drama. My biggest downfall is jumping in with both feet, right into someone else's business if I feel someone needs help. I absolutely hate bullying.

Labeling people is the number one reason why kids get bullied. If you aren't part of the in crowd, you're in the out crowd, which makes you an easy target.

I mean I don't usually go in throwing punches, but sometimes I have to. It's crossed my mind that I could totally get my ass kicked but I've been lucky so far. I'm a fighter when I have to be.

Wow...I sound like a total douche.

It's true though. I guess my mom is right, I'm a natural protector. I especially look after my friends. Since the beauty queens are a bit *wild and adventurous*, I must be the responsible one to make sure we don't get into trouble.

As much as I wish I were more care free of the consequences like the girls, I unfortunately think way too much about the "what ifs". Well...most of the time.

So...I'm the lucky one who keeps us in check. At least I try. There's only so much I can do.

Two

As I head to Mandy's room door to leave, I throw a makeup brush at Mandy.

"Hey...let's try and keep the dresses somewhat tame. You always find me really short dresses. I think my parents are starting to think I have night job."

"You have great legs woman! Why not show off one of your best assets. You don't like to display the "girls" so I'm left with working your legs."

"Well...not everybody is comfortable in their own skin like you. We don't all look as gorgeous as Mandy!"

Mandy sits up glaring at me, annoyed by my tone.

"Ugh...here we go again. Why are you always self-deprecating?"

"Wow...those are big word for you Mandy. Do you even know what it means?"

"Oh shut it. Listen to me. You are a hottie. No lie. It's written all over the fucking guys bathroom walls at school for Christ sake! I've seen it...don't ask."

I laugh as she gets up and grabs me by the arms with a look of desperation.

"Mia...you ARE beautiful." She says while playing with my hair.

"Wow...your hair is getting really long. It's almost past your ass now. I think it's time for a trim honey." she says while grabbing the ends of my hair. "Can we say "dead-ends".

I snatch my hair out of her hands and roll my eyes.

"No wonder why you can do so much with it. Its half fried." She teases.

"Maybe my hair is down to my ass so I can cover up the least pronounced good."

Mandy looks at me confused.

"My small ass Mandy."

Mandy falls over onto the bed laughing.

"Yeah...never mind. Don't cut it. Let it grow!"

"Wow. You're a jerk."

Mandy sits up with a smile.

"Oooh...Maybe we can buy you butt pads tomorrow!"

"Ha...ha...very funny. They don't even work."

Mandy looks at me with a quizzical brow.

"Hey...don't judge me. I bought some and it didn't look that great and..."

And there she goes, laughing hysterically.

"Oh...my...God... You actually bought some. I was totally messing with you. This...is greatness."

Mandy rolls back and forth laughing so hard she might actually pee herself.

"Okay. You officially suck ass. I'm leaving."

"Just leave the shopping up to me. And don't worry...I can work with your small ass." Mandy smiles dimpling her cheeks with her fingers.

Unfortunately for me, big butts are in these days. What we consider to be normal, is now small, and what we consider to be small is now practically pathetic. I'm not too far away from pathetic.

Tired of her jabs, I throw my backpack over my shoulder and wave a friendly goodbye with my middle finger.

I walk out of Mandy's house and start heading to my car, but I can't help the feeling of being watched. I turn back towards the house and look around the front porch and see nothing. Its only 7:30 p.m. but fairly dark outside. The rainy mist and cold air makes it seem like it's much later.

I look to my right...then left, still nothing. The neighborhood seems calm and quiet as usual.

Living in small town Silverton, Oregon, population less than 10,000, nothing exciting ever really happens here. Still...an eerie feeling has crept over me.

Everyone who lives in Silverton knows each other well, a little too well if you ask me. No secrets here. Silverton is only busy during the tourist season.

Silverton sits at the 45th parallel, 45 degrees north of the Earth's equatorial plane. Basically, everyone thinks Silverton lies as the halfway point between the equator and the north pole. Obviously, this is disputed by Scientists because based on the shape of the earth, this is technically not true, but Silverton takes full advantage of the tourist scam by putting up a sign marking the halfway point.

If you aren't at the local mom and pop shops or café's, you are taking an adventure through our state park to sight see our beautiful forests, waterfalls and creeks, or scoping out original architecture from the 1930's. Tourists season is typically during the summer or beginning of fall. The weather here is usually cold and damp, but we do tend to get quite a few beautiful sunshine days.

Even though I know crime here is little to nothing, I feel a presence. Something hiding in the dark. I don't feel scared, just curious.

I decide not to stand in the rain and get soaked, so I quickly head to the car. I open the door, jump in and start old blue.

Chill Mia. There's nothing out there.

I sit for a minute trying to calm my nerves. I turn on the heat and hold my hands up against the vents. After I thaw out a bit, I remember what I have to do.

Post Office.

Once my memory is jogged, I put the gear in drive and put the pedal to the medal, with a little hesitation from Old Blue.

I'm sure my poor little '83 Toyota Corolla has seen better days but even after more than 30 years, Old Blue still drives great...most of the time.

Old Blue was originally my Mom and Dad's car. My parents can totally afford to buy me a new car but I didn't want one. I've grown up in Old Blue and love it. All that matters is the AC, heater and radio still work. Essentially, I'm just happy to have my own car.

Besides, I'll be in on my way to College soon. What's the point of spending thousands of dollars on something I've only been using for two years.

I pull up next to the night drop-box at the local post office and pull out the sealed envelope my mother gave me this morning.

I glance at the address listed and see a name I'm not familiar with.

Dr. James Osborne
University of Cambridge – Ancient History Department
West Road
Cambridge
CB3 9EF, United Kingdom

Shrugging, I toss it in the box and drive off. Just another colleague of my parents I assume.

As long-time, esteemed historians for the prestigious Cambridge University, my parents have worked with many Professors.

I still wonder how my life would have turned out if I were raised in Great Brittan.

Luckily my parents were given the opportunity to work from home. With their expertise in antiquity, my parents negotiated a telecommuting contract with Cambridge under conditions that they report back to the University once a month and create an amiable workspace at home.

When we bought our home ten years ago, my parents did exactly what the University requested and much more.

Dad had a study and an archives room built which the University was more than willing to expense for research purposes. The study is what I call the "Museum" and the archives room, a.k.a. "Incubator", stores archeological findings and more than 100 relics in a temperature-controlled room. Sadly, I've never really paid too much attention to what my parents do besides look at really "old stuff".

Three

Within minutes I'm at the curb parking Old Blue. I turn it off, grab my backpack and books and jump out, realizing just how famished I am.

As I make my way up the walkway to the front door, eager to get out of this damp cold, I notice the door is open and hanging off the hinges.

My body tenses with an uneasy feeling but I run up the steps anyway.

"Mom? Dad? Is everything okay?"

As I step through the doorway, I'm shocked by the chaos.

Mom's favorite antique foyer table is turned over and broken in half, along with her shattered Oriental vase. Our grandfather clock looks like it was pushed over as well as our family photos that were hanging on the wall.

Following the chaos throughout the house, I see a trail of muddy footprints across the floor. As I follow the prints in confusion, I look up and see a crimson substance smudged against the wall.

I'm instantly frozen. I don't have to guess what it is.

My heart begins to race, and then jumps to overdrive.

Mom! Dad!

I drop my stuff and sprint to my left towards the formal living room in search of them.

"Mom!! Dad!! Where are you?!!"

I make my way across the hallway, past the staircase, into the kitchen and immediately halt at the horrific scene.

The shock has pulled the air from my lungs.

I stand there only momentarily before jumping over the puddle of blood to my mother. I drop to my knees and pull her head onto my lap, but see her dark empty eyes.

I try to cry out but my shattered, hoarse, voice stumbles.

My trembling hands try to shake her to get up.

"Mom! Please...please...oh God. No...mom. PLEASE!"

Her body is still warm, but I know she's gone.

I hug her hoping my love for her will awaken her.

As I cry over her, I look up and see my father's body by the dining table.

I gently lay my mother's head down and run to his body and see the same cold, distant, dark eyes.

"Dad...please. Get up...Dad..."

I know he's dead. They're both dead.

Oh God! What do I do?

I fall to the floor and pull my knees to my chest, using the kitchen island to hold me up.

Tears downpour like a waterfall. My head starts to spin and ache, and I become nauseated from the site of all the blood. Oddly I can smell the iron in it.

My stomach starts to heave but there's nothing there to vomit. I close my eyes and begin to take in deep breathes to make the nausea dissipate.

As my stomach calms, I slowly open my eyes and look down at my parents. The anguish I feel is unbearable and numbing at the same time.

Staring at their lifeless bodies I realize the cause of all the blood. Both of their throats have been slit. Knowing how they died makes me cry even harder.

But then, I quickly muffle myself with my hands, looking around in panicked fear that the murderer could still be in the house.

As I scan the room I halt when I see it. *The weapon.*

One of the kitchen knives is on the floor with a bloody towel wrapped around the handle.

I shudder, frightened by its sight. After God knows how long I finally reach into my pocket, pull out my cell, and dial 911.

***

"MIA! WAKE UP!"

I open my eyes to Bianca standing over me and I realize I'm in my dorm room. I must have finally fallen asleep.

I was dreaming of it again, replaying the events of that night.

I groggily sit up and look at my clock on the nightstand. It's 6:00 a.m. At least I got a few hours of sleep.

I sit there for a moment trying to rid my mind of the nightmare. I look down at myself and see that I'm drenched in sweat. My body feels like it's steaming with heat. Something I've encountered more and more lately, waking from sleep drenched in sweat and my body as hot as a furnace.

My senses are over stimulated and drained from such a realistic reencounter of that night and the reminiscence of blood. The scent and look of the thick substance still haunts me. My hands begin to tremble like they've been doing as of late after nightmares. A mere side effect of stress and anxiety I suppose.

I clutch my stomach and close my eyes trying to think of something else.

"Was it the same dream? The one about your parents?" Bianca asks.

"Yeah..."

"Oh Mia...are you okay? You look like your about to be sick?"

"I'm fine. I just...need a minute. I need to get up and shower."

Bianca rubs my back.

"Oh Mia, you are drenched and your body feels feverish love". Bianca says as she palms my head before walking back to her bed.

"Sorry I woke you."

"Hey...it's okay. I could hear you crying in your sleep. I woke you because I know how bad it can get for you. Besides, I need to get up anyway. I have an early class today. Are you sure you're okay? It's been over a year since you had a nightmare that bad. I mean I know you've had a few here and there in the last couple of months but this one seemed pretty bad. What do you think brought it all back up?"

I look at Bianca and pathetically shrug my shoulders.

"Yesterday was my Mom's birthday."

"Mia...why didn't you tell me? We could have done something. I'm so sorry."

"It's okay. I really didn't want to talk about it."

Bianca frowns and nods. She knows the truth about my parents. I confided in her after the nightmares woke her almost every other night the first couple of weeks into the first semester.

She's been a great friend to talk to, helping me get through it all – pushing me forward and never letting me dwell on it.

You would think a girl like Bianca would be a stuck-up snob with the way she looks. She's drop-dead gorgeous and the total opposite of what I perceived she would be. She's super sweet and down to earth, but does however, have quite the wild side.

Bianca is the only girl in her family of six and her parents love and spoil her rotten. Anything she wants she gets. Clothes, shoes, a brand-new car. Bianca was also one of the most loved and popular kids in high school. With all the glory in her life she's hardly known tragedy but somehow, she knows exactly what to do to help me get through mine.

"Okay...I've got to get up." Bianca jumps up to stretch. She yawns and I can't help but mimic her yawn.

We look at each other and both laugh at how yawning can create an involuntary trend.

Still utterly exhausted I just sit there while Bianca turns on her desk radio and starts to bounce to Panic at the Disco's *Girls Girls Boys*.

I laugh, watching her long shiny auburn pigtails bounce about.

I envy her beauty. Even just getting out of bed and wearing pajama shorts and a tank she looks great.

I was stunned by Bianca's perfection when we first met during freshman orientation. Insecurity crept over me when I saw her. Talk about feeling inadequate. Beautiful ivory complexion, honey brown eyes, thin yet *curvaceous in all the right places* figure - makes you sick with jealousy.

Looking down at my old warn out crop top t-shirt and boy shorts soaked from my night sweat terror, my lip curls in disgust. Just as I'm about to cover myself back up, Bianca grabs my hands, pulls me to stand, and twirls me around.
I laugh trying to steady myself.

"Wake up woman! Let's hit the showers and then grab a cup of Joe before class."

I nod approvingly and we gather our bath caddies and towels and head to the shower room.

Four

I have one more class before I head back to the dorm. Tonight, I start my new job.

When I ventured off campus yesterday to shop for toiletries, I saw a *HELP WANTED* sign on the door of a local coffee shop called *Mochas*. I immediately walked in and asked about it.

I don't need the money but figured it will keep me busy during my down time and my mind off certain...things. Since the Shop is open from morning to night there are plenty of hours to work if I get bored.

The Couple who own the shop, Mr. and Mrs. Taragos a.k.a. Mr. and Mrs. T., recently moved here. Super kind and sweet.

Mochas has only been open for a few months, but they are in desperate need of immediate assistance. They were so eager to have help that they asked if I could start moments after I interviewed.

Excited as I was to even get the job, I had to decline knowing I needed at least a day to get myself together,but suggested starting tonight.

Since my shift starts at 6:00 p.m. tonight and my upcoming class ends at 3:00 p.m., I should have enough time to do some homework before I clock in.

I walk in to English Lit and make my way up towards the back of the viewing gallery as usual. Most of the students sit within the first three rows but I like to keep a good distance from the chatter boxes, so I skip at least two rows behind them. I'm not necessarily an introvert but I like to stay focused.

I take a seat at the end of the aisle and pull out my book, notepad, and pen.

Professor Stevens walks in and begins his lecture, discussing early 18th century literature. The subject brings back one of the best memories I have. My sixteenth birthday.

Mom hands me a large wrapped box. I begin unwrapping the box excruciatingly slow, amused by her impatience. I watch her watching me, waiting for my reaction. As I tear off the last part of the wrapping paper and open the box, I gasp at the lineup of books. Pride and Prejudice by Jane Austen, First Edition. I can't believe it. The set must have cost a fortune. Crying and laughing at the same time I jump and hug her, embracing her soothing lavender vanilla smell.

"I know Pride and Prejudice is your favorite and I love that it's your favorite because it used to be mine as well at your age." She says while wiping away my tears.

"You remind me of Elizabeth. You have her strength, courage, whit, and generous heart. And you always want to help those in need, one of your best qualities. If I suddenly leave this world, I know in my heart that you will do great things. You are special Mia. You'll understand just how special you really are in time. Happy Birthday my love."

I close my eyes hoping and praying the tears don't trickle down as they begin to water from the memory.

My body begins to tremor as usual when I get upset, and I begin to feel the rooms temperature rise.

Startled by the Professors amplified voice as he describes his passion for Literature, I jump back into reality and my body begins to cool as I slow my breathing. Any time I begin to feel an anxiety attack coming I close my eyes and slowly breathe in and out until I refocus myself.

I see the rest of the students open their notepads preparing to jot down notes, so I follow, but notice my pen is missing.

Sure that I pulled one out, I search the floor for where it could be.

Just as I'm about to grab my bag to search for another one, an adjacent voice startles me.

"Are you looking for this? I believe it rolled off your desk."

I look over to my left frightened and surprised to see a hand held out, holding my pen.

I follow the hand upward and I'm suddenly hypnotized by piercing sapphire blue eyes.

I unintentionally hold my breath, fixated by his gaze and what seems to be an invisible grasp. I scan over his features. His perfect masculine a-lined jaw, hidden beneath a five o'clock shadow...leading up to a clean edged-retro twirled raven black mess...and those eyes, those hypnotic blue eyes.

He holds my gaze, watching me take him in. When I look back to the sapphire jewels, he suddenly disengages, and quickly turns away.

His brows furrow and jaw tightens in what I believe to be agitation, waiting for me to take the pen. His sudden transition diverts me, and I shake free from the reverie.

Flushing from embarrassment I clumsily grab my pen.

"Um...thank you."

"My pleasure," he replies with a deep sultry accent. Not sure if its English or something else.

I hurriedly lean back into my seat and look down at my notepad aggravated with myself.

Where did he come from?

I didn't even know he was there this whole time. I don't remember seeing anyone come up to sit close to me.

Holy shit! He's hot. I think I irritated him by the dumb look on my face. *Idiot!* I act like I've never seen a hot guy before.

Tempted to look up at him to see if he's looking back at me, I think...better not.

Concentrate!

I dart my eyes forward towards the Professor and do my best to focus on his lecture. The more I try to concentrate the more I can't help but think about those penetrating eyes. I fidget over and over trying to get comfortable and trying to compose the heat my body suddenly feels.

I glance towards him, hiding beneath my lashes and see him smirking. *Okay Dickhead.*

Annoyed, I roll my eyes. *Of course.* I'm sure he's enjoying my reaction. He must be one of those guys who knows he's hot and takes full advantage of his effect on women. *Ass!*

The Professor continues to lecture while I undesirably, secretly, admire *Mr. Hottie.*

He leans back relaxed in his chair looking oh so suave. His long-sculpted torso stooping low against the seat, barely hidden under his fitted white T. Resting his elbow on the chair table, I watch as he swirls his chin back and forth around his knuckles.

My eyes trace up and down his body and I notice that his jeans are hanging *oh so low. Oh my.*

I inhale deeply and then release imagining he has that sexy V. Why am I hot for this guy right now? I can't seem to control myself.

Almost sensing my wonder, he slightly shifts his head towards me, peering down at me, and grins.

I immediately look straight, my breath hitched, knowing I was caught.

Damn it!

Annoyance and anger builds deep within me again, feeling as if he's sitting there so perfectly on purpose.

Ugh!!

"I look forward to reviewing your assignments. Any questions? No? Great! Class dismissed!"

Oh thank the Universe! I don't know how much longer I can sit here feeling vulnerable.

I quickly gather my book and notepad and shove them in my bag.

I stand holding my pen tight from the anxiety of wanting to see him face to face.

Wait. Where did he go?

I look down towards the other end of the aisle and then at the front of the class and there's no sign of him.

How did he get out of here so fast?

I must have missed him leaving when I was putting my stuff up.

As much as I'm relieved that the intensity between us is gone, I'm a little disappointed that he left so quickly.

I jog down the aisle frustrated and head for the door. As I turn out of the doorway, I collide with what feels like a brick wall.

I start to fall back, but I'm suddenly caught by two strong arms.

I look up and Mr. Hottie is staring down at me holding me at my waist.

Five

"Shit! I mean...sorry." Once I steady myself Mr. Hottie lets go of me.

Looking up at the massive tower standing in front of me, I'm in awe. He must be at least 6'2 because I barely stand level with his shoulders.

"I'm terribly sorry. Are you alright?" He asks.

Okay...I am totally digging the accent. I can't quite grasp where he might be from. At this point I don't care.

"Oh...umm...yeah. I'm fine. Sorry. I didn't see you."

Mr. Hottie smirks and then looks down at the ground. He slowly bends down to pick up my pen I dropped, *again*, but steadies his gaze on me.

My stomach flutters from the intense vibe I'm getting, and my heart is pounding at high speed.

I bite my lip and look away feeling self-conscious.

When he stands, he hands me the pen and I quickly take it, aggravated by my insecurity.

"Thanks."

"You're welcome. Maybe you should put some glue on that."

I look up at him and he looks away gloating from his smartass remark.

"Very funny." I say sneering.

"You're in quite the hurry." He says.

"What gave me away? Bolting full throttle into a brick wall you call a chest? You know you should really stay off the Roids. I could have knocked myself out." I say irritated by his confidence.

He's still smirking at me and its driving me crazy.

Damn that sexy smirk.

"Well...I did catch you."

"What a gentleman." I say curtly.

"I try." He says as he puts his hand over his chest.

His gorgeous eyes staring right into mine makes my irritation float away. When I finally break his hold by looking down at my pen I remember where I was heading in such a hurry.

"I better get going. In a hurry remember. I gotta get to the campus office before it closes."

"I'm heading that way. I'll walk with you if you don't mind?"

He puts his hand out in front of me ready to introduce himself. "I'm Alex."

I look up at the glistening sincerity in his eyes and take his hand in mine.

"Mia."

"Nice to meet you Mia. Please...lead the way."

And then the cocky smirk is back.

I narrow my eyes wondering what game he's playing when I see him trying to hide a laugh.

"I promise...I won't bite."

The grin across his face is just too much. I feel like he knows something I don't.

"Well...I just might. I would keep a good distance."

Now I'm being cocky. Alex throws his hands up giving in to my warning.

Alex and I walk in silence, glancing at one another here and there, both not knowing what to say. Alex gets this look like something might come out but he can't find the words. I finally give in and start talking.

"So...are you new to Duke? I don't think I've ever seen you in Literature class before."

"Actually, I'm just visiting. Observing really." He says casually.

"Oh?" *Observing?*

Alex looks amused.

"I'm an old benefactor for the University. I'm just making sure funding is being put to good use."

Benefactor? He looks my age or maybe a couple of years older than me but not old enough to be a *Benefactor*.

"I assume you were once a student then? Alumni?"

"Yes. I graduated some time ago. I have an MBA and a PHD in Cultural History."

History? That feels to close to home. I think my sudden solemnness washes over me because Alex's smile fades.

"You must not be a fan of History."

"Oh no. I...you...you just don't look much older than me and you already have your PHD. That's pretty amazing."

"I'm older than you think." Alex says laughing.

"Well you age well."

Alex puts his hand on his chest and smirks at me.

"Why is that a compliment?" He teases.

"Merely an observation. Don't let it go to your head."

"I'll do my best." He says smiling.

We walk up to the office and Alex again looks like he's struggling with something. Before I can ask him what he's thinking I'm distracted by a tall, broad shouldered man, with what looks to be tribal tattoos running up his neck to his half shaven Mohawk skull, staring at me from the office. We make direct eye contact a rigid, disturbing grin spreads across his face.

The man's expression suddenly turns dark, as if he's angry. Not anger towards me but towards someone standing next to me.

When I turn to look at Alex to see if he's seeing what I'm seeing, Alex is glaring at the man, and for a moment, I'm frightened by what I see.

Alex's jaw tightens and the look of disgust is written all over his face.

"Do you know that guy?" I ask timidly.

"No." he says curtly.

I turn back towards the office watching the man make his way towards the office exit door and something tells me I should get out of here before he comes out. I look up to tell Alex we should leave but I'm astonished by his disappearance. Alex is nowhere to be found. I look up and down the hallways and again no Alex.

I turn back to face Mohawk guy who was coming my way and he too is gone. I twirl in a semi-circle confused, wondering if I've gone mad because no one is around.

What the...

I walk into the office and see the office secretary Linda sitting at her desk.

"Hey Linda...uhm...do you know the guy that was just in here?"

Linda stares at me like she's day dreaming.

"What guy?"

"The one with the tattoos that was just in here?"

Linda looks lost in thought and then finally breaks herself from what may have been a daydream. When she finally comes to, she acts as if I just came in the office.

"Hey Mia. How are you today?" she says with such perkiness.

"Uhm...I'm fine. Are you okay?"

"Oh yes dear...I'm doing quite well."

Okay...this is totally weird.

"Alright then...I was actually stopping by to give you the flyer you asked me to create for your Book Club Night." I pull out the flyer and hand it over to her.

As Linda looks over the flyer I glance around the hallway and down the office corridors and no sign of Alex or Mohawk guy. So strange.

"I would stay and chat but I gotta go. I hope the flyer looks okay."

"Oh it's wonderful! You did great. Thank you dear." She says with glee.

"Great. Well I'll email you the electronic version and...see you later Linda. Bye."

"Bye hone!"

I walk out of the office still searching for Alex and there's no sign of him or anyone else for that matter. *WTF?*

Making my way down the hall I suddenly start to panic by the hallways emptiness, and the feeling of being alone quickly makes me nervous. The grin on Mohawk guy gave me the creeps.

I decide to jog down the hallway, trying to get to the exit door and out to open grounds as quickly as possible. Being in an empty hallway is exactly how scary movies start out. *No thanks.*

The campus usually shuts down pretty early until night classes, so no one is around after 3:00p.m. I finally slow down and stop to lean up against the wall trying to understand what just happened.

"What the hell? It's lack of sleep. I'm losing it due to insomnia." I tell myself. Too tired to think straight I walk out the exit door and head to the dorm.

Six

Back in my dorm I flop down on my bed and take in the long day. It's already three thirty and I have homework to do. I pull out my assignments and books and head to my desk.

Sitting there my mind wanders to *Mr. Hottie*. He probably snuck away to save himself from my company. Didn't seem very interested.

He's probably a total ass anyway. Too hot to be a nice guy. And who the hell was the Mohawk guy? He looked like he could be on *America's Most Wanted*.

Remembering the way Mohawk guy grinned at me makes my skin crawl. Hoping to shake him from my mind, I pull out my homework assignment and begin researching Ancient Greek Mythology. I don't have time to figure out what just happened. I barely have enough juice in me to keep up with school and work. I need to focus on what's right in front of me.

Just as I'm about to bury myself into the history of the early Roman Empire, my cell rings. It's Mandy.

Shit!

I haven't spoken to Mandy in months. Actually, since before school started this year. We've text back and forth but I just haven't had the courage to hear her voice. It reminds me too much of home.

I try to cut ties from home. Just last week I decided to turn my cell back on after being off for months. I was getting calls from everyone in the neighborhood nearly every month asking how I was doing, and it was driving me insane. I didn't want to talk about it nor get the pity party.

I know Mandy is my best friend, but I need room to breathe. I think about denying her call but I really do miss her. I decide to give in.

"Hey Mandy."

"Mia! Finally! I've been trying to get in touch with you for months!! I can't believe you actually answered. I mean I'm glad you did. So... how's like as a Junior? Tell me everything.? Have you made any new best friends this year? Have you hooked up with any guys yet? Are your Professors hot? And why haven't you CALLED ME?!!!" She probes almost crying.

I shake my head at her interrogation.

"Alright...let's calm down. One question at a time. Nothing really anything exciting to report. Every day is pretty much the same." *Except for Mr. Hottie.* "I've made friends here and there in class, and you know about my roommate Bianca. Don't worry, you can never be replaced. No wild hook ups or hook ups at all. No...none of my Professors are hot. Gross! And...I'm sorry I haven't called." I can almost hear the disappointment in her silence.

"Mia...how are you really doing? I still can't get over how fast you booked it from home. You barely speak to anyone from Silverton and you don't come home during the summer or holiday breaks. You really didn't give yourself enough time to really grieve before going to College. I know it's been three years, but I worry about you. I always call but it goes straight to voicemail. I mean I know we text here and there but it's not the same. Sometimes I wonder if I'll ever hear from you again. It's like you ran away from us all." She sighs waiting for my response.

"I'm sorry. I just...had to get away. I couldn't be there any longer.

I turn my phone off sometimes to avoid all the pity checkups. I don't come home during the summer or holiday breaks because I'm not ready to face home again. And I just didn't want to talk about it anymore. I needed distance and time."

"Well I think you got distance covered. You're in freaking North Carolina! You're all the way on the other side of the continental U.S.! Why didn't you pick Stanford or even San Diego? We could have been roommates here in San Diego!" She says exasperated.

"Mandy...I really do miss you. I just need to focus on me. I want to graduate and get my life started. I'm sorry. I don't want you to worry. I'm fine." Tears begin to run down my face. "I can't thank you and your family enough for helping me get through the worst time of my life. Your mom has always been like a second mother to me and she is my home away from home. I miss her...and her Tamales." We both giggle.

"But right now, I need to be on my own and alone. As much as I wanted to stick around to figure out why and who, I knew if I did, I would never leave it alone and I would forever be consumed by it. My parents wouldn't want that for me. Besides...Sheriff Daniels has done everything he can. It's a little hard when there's not much to go by. No finger prints, no witnesses, only a set of boot prints, what else could he really do." I choke back the hesitation in my voice.

"You mean two?"

"Two what?" I whisper.

Mandy silences as if she's given something away.

"Didn't the Sheriff tell you? So my mom saw Sheriff Daniels a month ago outside the grocery store and you know those two, chatty Kathy's. The Sherriff told her that they discovered there were ac-tually two separate boot prints. Meaning there were two intruders. Not just one. The Sheriff said the crazy thing is the forensics team told the Sheriff that it looked like the two intruders got into a scuffle or something. It took months for him to get results back from Portland.

"I don't understand. Why didn't the Sheriff tell me? I told him to notify me of anything and everything they find."

"I don't know. I know he got the final results back some time after we left for College. I figured he would have called you by now. He may have tried but your phone was off. Mia I'm sorry to bring all this up. I didn't want to call and talk about that. I'm super excited for how far you've come...and so proud. I hope you know you didn't let your parents down." She sighs.

I'm silent trying to process the new information.

"So what does he think it means? That someone tried to fight the murderer off? So does that mean someone else was there that night and hasn't come clean about it?"

"I don't know Mia. Look, you must have a ton of work to do. I just wanted to call and see how you're doing and know that you are alive. I was so worried about you. You have no idea. If it weren't for the Sheriff confirming with Duke you were attending classes, I would have taken off and hunted you down."

"I know. I'm sorry. I uhm actually...start my new part-time job in a few hours."

"What?! Mia!" She scolds me.

"Why would you add a part time job to your plate? You have enough going on. You don't need the money. Your parents made sure of that."

"I know. It's not about the money. Besides...it might help me meet new people." I sigh looking at the clock realizing we've been on the phone for a while.

"Hey...I'm sorry but I better go Mandy. I have homework to do before I clock in." It's my excuse to get off the phone.

"Okay. I love and miss you Mia. I'm here for you. And don't forget to call my mom. She worries about you and she misses you too."

"I will. I love and miss you too. Next time we'll talk about you and San Diego I promise. Gotta go...bye." My voice strained

"Bye Mia." Her tone sincere.

I wipe away the tears and suddenly feel angry as I think about the Sheriff. *Why didn't he leave a message with the Dorm?*

It's been three years! Why am I just now learning about this?

I pick up my cell and see that it's already fifteen after four. Knowing I've got a lot to do, I decide to hold off on calling the Sheriff to scold him until tomorrow.

I just can't believe someone else was there. The idea that someone else was there, maybe even trying to help gives me hope that the Sheriff might find something to lead us to their murderer. I just don't understand why this mysterious person hasn't come forward with information, or even made an anonymous tip.

The first couple of months after the murder were rough for me. I didn't eat or sleep much and all I thought about was finding who did it. I harassed the Sheriff daily with calls and visits. I hired a PI and researched local convicts. I became obsessed.

My obsession with finding the killer was so bad that I actually put myself in danger following a lead to Portland. I ended up in the wrong part of Portland and had to quickly get myself out. The Sheriff found out after I accidently opened my big mouth about it, so he had a uniform tail me every day after. Once I left Silverton, it was like the obligation to solve my parents' case was lifted. I was too far away and too busy to make a difference.

Though, the more I think about it now, the more anxious I become. That drive to find information begins to tingle in my fingertips.

And the anger I suddenly feel from the Sheriffs lack of communication begins to boil inside me. My body feels like it's going to set itself on fire so much so that I begin to shake.

Knowing I'm about to get another anxiety attack I quickly begin my breathing therapy. Slowly in and out until I find my inner peace. While I continue my breathing technique, I set it in my mind to let it all go for now and get back to what I have control over.

After a little over an hour of homework, I close my books and put my assignments up in my bag. I somehow managed to complete all my homework and I have about half an hour before my shift begins.

I decide to change into something a little more comfortable for a long night. I take off my blue blouse and put on a plaid button up. I keep my skinny jeans on as they've already stretched to perfect form. I kick off my flats and jump into my Toms.

I go to the mirror to give myself a quick look over and see the tired rings around my big gray eyes. I grab my cover up and dab it under my eyes, pull my hair up into a high bun, run a little gloss over my lips, take one last look at myself and shrug in fair content.

Crap! Now I have twenty minutes. I grab my shoulder bag and head out the door.

Seven

It's almost closing time and I'm beat. Learning to make a variety of caffeinated drinks isn't as easy as I thought it would be. Thankfully Mrs. T created a cheat sheet for me.

It's taking me a little longer to figure out all of the different names and meanings of caffeinated beverages but I'm predicting to be a pro by next millennia.

"Mia...you okay to close up tonight? I need to run by the grocery store for the Mrs. before I go home."

"Sure. We only have an hour before closing and I don't see us being bombarded with customers this late." I look out the shop windows and see the empty dark street ahead.

I really hope no one comes by.

"If you tell me what I need to do, I will take it from here."

"Thank you so much Mia." He pats my shoulder gently and begins to explain closing procedures.

Mr. T is beyond sweet and kind. His gentle smile brings about this light within him that makes it hard to not love the guy.

His rich and thick accent is something to appreciate. He purposefully and slowly annunciates each English word which reminds me of voice recordings my parents use to listen to of a Professor from East Europe describing various archeological findings.

As a child I would mock his pronunciation of words, not be cruel, but because I loved the way he spoke.

I think that's why I enjoy conversing with Mr. T. That, and he's been very patient with me during this entire learning process.

I mean I already owe him likely my first day of pay since I ruined a few pots of their very expensive Arabic coffee.

I read the measurements from Mrs. T's cheat sheet wrong and made the coffee so strong that not even a gallon of water could have saved the batches. I finally got the gist of it after the third bad batch.

"You know...you remind me of my grandmother. She had your same spirit. Her perseverance and drive was like no other. When she was determined to do something, no one could get in her way. You have that same drive Mia. You made a few mistakes here and there today, which is absolutely normal for someone with no experience, but you pushed through and didn't allow your mistakes to falter your ability to continue on and learn. Don't ever lost that drive Mia."

Mr. T. smiles and grabs my chin the way my father use to. It's endearing.

"That's very kind of you to say. Please do dock my pay for those mistakes." I say embarrassed.

"No...no...not necessary. When we first bought this shop, I made many mistakes as well. The Mrs. Would not leave me alone for more than five minutes knowing I would screw something up."

We both laugh.

"Would it be rude of me to ask what your ethnicity is Mr. T.?"

"Of course not. We are Romani. Very proud Roma." He says with a smile.

I think back to the time I first learned about the Roma culture. It was when I first read The Hunchback of Notre Dame. I was 11 years old.

In the book, the term Gypsy was used as a derogatory form for people of the Roma culture.

I remember asking my parents what Gypsy's were and my father ever so kindly explained to me the origin of that term and the sadness it created for the Romani people.

My father explained that Romani people were discriminated against for living a nomadic lifestyle, constantly on the move. They were persecuted as cunning, mysterious thieves.

However, Romani people believe in family, respect, honor and justice. They believe in a worldview of *Rromano*, which means to behave with dignity and respect.

Knowing that Mr. and Mrs. T are Romani makes me love them even more.

"Do you know about the Roma culture Mia?"

"A little. Only what my father told me. He told me about the origin of the Roma culture and the unfortunate prejudice Romani people endured for centuries. And he also taught me that Romani people are no different than any other person, and that each person, no matter their origin, should be judged by their own actions and behavior."

For a brief moment, Mr. T.'s eyes water. He smiles and nods his head.

"Your father sounds like he was an amazing man."

Was?

Before I can ask how he knew, Mr. T says a quick goodbye and walks out the door. As if he was hiding some raw emotion that needed to be released in private.

It was then, that the shop's deafening silence hits me. I haven't really talked about my father with anyone. I miss him so much.

My father was as kind as Mr. T. and was loved by everyone. I can't recall one bad memory of my father. He was patient when I was reckless, he was forgiving when I was forbidding.

He had so much faith in me and what I would become.

I begged the Universe to never let me fail him. I could never forgive myself if I was ever the cause of him losing confidence in me that no other person on earth could ever possess. I was my father's world.

As much as I want to cry thinking about him, I smile instead. I think about all the crazy things I did as a kid and how I terrified him sometimes. I had no fear as a child.

I never feared heights so I would climb the highest tree or house rooftop. I had no fear of water so I would dive into pools with no floats even at five years old and didn't know how to swim.

At age seven I had no concept of what might happen if I skateboarded down a steep hill, that was also a busy street with no pads or helmet.

My father caught me every time I was seeking what I saw as a new adventure and the near heart attack's I gave him was unforgettable. He would hug me so tight I thought he would never let me go.

I miss those hugs. I miss him thinking he could have lost me. It's almost ironic. His biggest fear was losing me, and I was the one that ended up losing him.

I wish I knew why. Why anyone would want to take his life? He was the most deserving human being to live a full and happy life.

Sulking against the counter I remember my conversation with Mandy. I must know what the Sherriff found. Who else was there that night?

I go over that night in my head and in my dreams often. I remember being on the phone with my mother only a brief time before she was gone. I should have told her how much I loved and appreciated her. She deserved to know how amazing she was.

I always wonder what would have happened if I didn't go to the post office that night. Would I have died too? Or would I have been able to scare the intruder off and save my parents.

I don't know if the Universe has a purpose for us all or if things really do happen for a reason. Honestly, I don't know what I believe in.

I don't know if there is a God, but if there is one, I hope he or she knows how special my parents are, and how lucky he or she is to have two amazing souls in heaven.

Eight

"He's found her." I growl.

"We knew it wouldn't take long brother. I'm guessing he was just as surprised to see you as you him. How did your little chat go with the old Brut?"

Lucius sits on the edge of the building top cleaning his Gladius as usual while we keep watch.

"There wasn't much to discuss seeing how I didn't give him an opportunity."

As soon as Brutus saw me with Mia. He knew the only way to get to her is to first go through me. I countered his draw and tempted him to follow me down to the basement. My movement was far too fast for Mia to see and her distraction of my disappearance allowed Brutus the opportunity to escape her view. As soon as he was down the stairs, I lunged at him and held him captive to the wall by his throat.

"You are not welcome here Brutus." I said with ferocity.

"The Council has ordered me to bring her in." he squeels.

I tighten my grip on his throat only allowing him to speak through a frail voice.

"No. She is not theirs to have."

"You think you and little brother will be able to protect her?

They will all come for her. If not the Council, the others will. We all feel her power growing. None of us have ever felt this connection before. Let the Council handle her. We will all be better off for it."

"She remains under our protection. Her power may be growing but it is still dormant. I will not let her be taken and caged like a rat for science."

"The Council wishes her no harm. They merely want to protect her from herself."

"And I'm supposed to believe this after they murdered the other Saga's? Including Mia's mother? What do you think she will do once she finds out? Do you really think she will trust The Council?"

"There's no proof that the Council had anything to do with that."

"I see. And three years ago? I was there that night. I'm the one that eliminated the mongrel that killed her parents. You expect me to believe he wasn't there on The Council's order?"

"Must have been a stray. The Council would have sent me to retrieve her, not some vagrant."

"This is a final warning Brutus. Tell the Council she is under my protection and I will do whatever necessary to keep her safe."

"You are way over your head Alexander. You won't be able to control her."

"I do not intend to control her. She is under my guard and if The Council comes for her again, I will let loose upon them like a plague. Much like I did in 1665. You remember don't you?" I say through gritted teeth.

I release Brutus and shove him back. He snarls at me and just as he gets ready to pounce on me, we hear students come down the stairs."

"I wouldn't make a spectacle Brutus. Wouldn't want The Council hearing about it."

"This isn't over Alexander."

"Oh I think it is Brutus. Be sure to give The Council my message." I say as I walk away and head up the stairs.

I was ready to snap his neck in two right then and there. The thought of Brutus touching Mia made me want to rip him limb from limb.

"Brutus has never been one for light conversation brother. He forgets his manners. Can't teach an old dog new tricks." Lucius says laughing.

"I am curious as to what you were thinking when you decided to make an entrance into her life. We've always stayed in the shadows while protecting the Saga's. We've only made ourselves known when they absolutely needed us."

Something has drawn me to her. More so than the other Saga's.

"I felt her energy the other night. I know you did as well. It's awakening in her. The stronger it gets the easier it will be for the others to find her. She's been holding back her grief from the loss of her parents far too long. Do you remember what happened to Genevieve when her child was taken away? Her grief and anger consumed her. Though the Vis was passed down, Saga's always have power lingering within them. Mia's power is far greater than Genevieve's. She could be the one to end us all or, set us free."

What is true freedom? We've never known such thing. Lucius and I have been a part of this dark world far longer than we ever hoped to be. We grew up in a time when men were slaves to the wealthy and when the Army could take you from your home at any time if they needed numbers. Didn't matter the age as long as you could wield a sword. Lucius and I never knew true freedom until Selene gave us this gift. At least that's what we thought.

Our kind is not immortal. We do age, though it takes hundreds of years to see a difference, and our kind can be killed. But not Lucius and I. We are forever cursed to live. We do not have the same weaknesses as most of our kind. Selene granted us the ability to withstand any danger we faced in order to protect her bloodline. The Council has ordered our deaths many times over but our strength, speed and ability to regenerate is unmatched. Though, we finally came to realize we were just recruited to another set of chains. What we would give to be free of this eternal life of servitude.

"That is exactly why the Council will do anything to take her life. They don't want her Vis getting out of hand. She holds the power to destroy our kind. They also want to be in control of when and whom she passes her Vis to."

The thought of anyone touching Mia to produce a child has me enraged. My hands form into fists and I feel by blood scorching. I must not think of it.

"Do you fear her the way the others do" I ask Luscious.

"Fear her for being able to break us of this "forever"? No brother. We've lived through man's greatest and foulest moments in life. I do not fear death. I use to long for it honestly. Now, I am content with either living or seeing the end."

I contemplate what Luscious said. I remember the time when he longed for death. He had lost hope in humanity and hope in our purpose. When you live as long as we have, you see far more tragedies than miracles. Every moment humanity takes a step forward, they seem to then take two steps back.

Humans feel a sense of release when they hate. We've sadly seen the desolate caves of mans darkest souls and it never ceases to amaze us.

When Lucius met Cassandra is 1922, his love for humanity changed. He fell madly in love with her and she helped him see man's ability for compassion. Before she passed in 1958 from cancer, she asked that he live a life of compassion instead of abhorrence. It changed him for the better.

Cassandra was certainly his most memorable love and thankfully his saving grace. It was hard to be there and have all the answers for Lucius when I didn't have the answers for myself. The why's to our existence and purpose. But Mia has changed something in me. I can't stop thinking about her. I'm drawn to her and being away from her makes me ache inside, an ache I've never felt before. I will do whatever it takes to protect her, even if it means crossing the line.

"Where are you going brother?" Lucius asks.

"I don't like her being out this late. I just saw Taragos leave the shop. I'm going to get a closer look and ensure she is safe."

"Brother...you are stepping over the line here. You're getting too close to this one. You remember how you were with Genevieve. You nearly collapsed a city with your rage from what happened to her."

I ignore Lucius and leap down to the ground. I look up and see Lucius still sitting and cleaning his sword and shaking his head at me.

"Yes...yes...I'll be watching. Try not to have too much fun brother." Lucius says.

Nine

As I wash the cups that have piled up in the sink, I hear the doorbell chime. *Ugh*. Of course. Right before closing time.

"I'll be right with you." I shout.

I quickly rinse the cups and put them on the small drying rack. I grab a clean towel and begin drying my hands.

I turn around and I'm instantly frozen in place. Mr. Hottie is sitting at the bar in front of me just staring.

I stand stunned for a moment then I quickly take out my notepad and pen from my apron and walk towards him.

"Hello Mia. I didn't know you worked here."

"Sorry to disappoint."

"That's not what I meant. I must apologize for suddenly running off on you. I saw... one of the professors I was looking for. He was heading down the basement stairs and I needed to catch him before I left. By the time I came back you were already gone. I did tell you I would be right back."

"I didn't hear you say anything."

"My sincerest apologies. I should have made sure you heard me. That was rude of me."

I'm not sure whether I believe him but the look of sincerity in his perfect sapphire eyes makes me feel like I don't care.

"Well...how can I help you?" dropping my gaze down to my notepad.

"A cup of decaff please." he asks sweetly.

I look up and his eyes are still focused on me. Once again, I'm overcome by his utter perfection.

I break eye contact and turn around to walk to the premade coffee pot. "Coming right up." I say sheepishly.

Feeling as if his eyes are burning through me, my hands shake as I fetch a cup and pour the coffee. My nerves are completely rattled.

I close my eyes and take in one deep breath and slowly release as I open them. *He's just a guy. A really hot guy!*

I shake the thought from my mind and grab a saucer for the cup and a spoon for stirring.

I slowly turn around, concentrating on not spilling the coffee. I gently put the coffee on the counter and push it to Alex.

As I'm about to turn back around to escape him, he startles me once again.

"May I please have some cream and sugar?"

Doh! Of course. I should have remembered to ask.

"Of course."

I reach under the bar for the Sugar dispenser, open the small refrigerator underneath, and pull out the creamer.

When I bring them up, I clumsily hit the side of the bar with the sugar dispenser. Ignoring my idiocy, I set both down in front of him.

"Here you go. Sorry I didn't ask." Looking down shaking my head at my manners.

"Please...no apology needed." He says sincerely.

The awkwardness I feel is overbearing. I just want to escape him. I feel like a clumsy idiot around him. I'm sure he thinks so too.

"Are you here alone?" he asks with a perplexed look as he scans the place.

"Um yes. Mr. T...the owner... just left about ten minutes ago."

"It's really late for you to be here alone. Is he not fearful of your safety? You never know who could walk in." he says with what sounds like concern.

I honestly didn't think about the late hour or my safety until just now. *Thank you very much.* That was *creepy.*

I look out the shop windows taking in how dark it really is outside and then look back at *Alex* who's holding his cup mid-air, pressing his lips together as if he's trying to hide a smile.

I narrow my eyes at him in his attempt to alarm me.

"Thank you for your concern but I can take care of myself." I scold.

"And with all due respect, shouldn't you be concerned with your own safety? After all, you are the one out and about this late hour. Also...I sort of got a "creeper" vibe from your questioning. Are you trying to give me a hint?"

He looks up at me trying to hold back a laugh and holds my gaze.

"I didn't mean to offend you or *creep* you out Mia. I just think it would be a good idea to have more than one person closing at such a late hour. You never know what strange creatures might be lurking around at this time." He says playfully.

"Like possums?" I ask quizzically.

Alex laughs.

"Yeah. Those things are scary. Vicious little fanged creatures."

The look on Alex's face seems a little sad by my remark.

"Right...well...I better get back to cleaning. I'll be closing up shortly."

"Am I keeping you?"

"Oh...no. I wasn't trying to kick you out. You have plenty of time. Customers come first." I return a quick smile and begin wiping down the counter with a wash cloth.

After a few moments I decide to break the awkward silence.

"So...you never did finish telling me about your time at Duke.

History major right?" I say trying to think of something to talk about.

"Yes. At least one of my majors. I also majored in Business. You can never go wrong with a degree in business." he says with a smirk.

"True. It seems like you can use the degree for just about anything." I concede.

He smiles. "Maybe so. How do you like it so far at Duke?"

"So far so good." I shrug.

"Have you decided on a major?" he asks intently interested.

"No...not yet." I glance up and I'm caught by his beauty once more. The energy between us seems to electrify me.

The moment seems to last forever, and I finally take in a breath. I fidget trying to gain back my senses.

"Do I make you uncomfortable?" he asks gracefully.

Shocked by the question I look down at the counter and wait a moment before I answer.

"Nooo." *Liar!*

"Okay...maybe."

"It's hard to get an idea of what you're thinking...that's all. The way you look at me..." I say trying to come up with an excuse.

"Well I doubt most people know what I'm thinking unless their mind readers." He says jokingly.

"Very funny. I'm serious. You look at me as if you can see through me. It can be a little intense." I say.

"Intense? Maybe I find you attractive Mia."

Wow.

The sensual way he said that made my stomach dive and my knees weak. I start getting this tingling feeling between my thighs.

Staring into his eyes I feel like there's something pulling me in and I can't escape it. I think he feels it too because we can't seem to break free from it.

"See...there you go again. I feel like I'm a dear in headlights. Though I'm sure you have that effect on all women."

Alex smirks but says nothing.

Yup! He's a hottie whore.

"So...what do you do Alex?" I ask interested, leaning over the counter with my arms crossed.

I refuse to let Mr. Hottie be the one in control here with his charm and good looks.

"I have my hand in a few things. Stock markets. Real Estate." He says submitting to my change of topic.

"Interesting. Sounds like your Duke education has worked out well for you."

I'm flirting now. It's hard not to. And at least I feel in control.

"Seems so."

"Business must be a little hard with this economy though."

"True. The economy has taken its toll however I'm quite the entrepreneur." He says sneeringly.

I giggle a little to myself thinking about Mr. Hottie's business savvy and negotiating skills. I bet he can get whatever he wants.

He cocks his head to the side amused.

"What's so funny?"

"Oh nothing...you just seem like a guy who gets whatever he wants." I'm shocked by my own confession.

"Why do you say that?" he asks with a sexy smirk.

Why did I say that? Damn it!

Regretting that last statement I lift myself up from the counter flushed.

"Oh...Just an observation."

"Great education remember?" He says stirring his coffee.

"Of course." Now I'm smirking.

Ten

"So. How long have you worked here?"

"First day on the job."

"I bet you're a highly acclaimed Barista by now." he says jokingly.

"I am." I say sarcastically giving a curtsey.

Were back to flirting.

"I would whip you up a spectacular non-fat Latte with my awesome skills but unfortunately closing time is near." I respond acting like I'm looking at my watch.

"How about tomorrow?" his says soft and sweet.

"What?" I say confused.

Alex stares at me and my stomach tightens from the sensuality of it. I pull from his gaze and look down.

"Are you working tomorrow?" he asks.

"Yes." I say instantly.

"Tomorrow then." He says with such an angelic look.

He sits the coffee cup down and stands, reaches into his pocket and pulls out his wallet. Flipping through his wallet I can't help but check out the whole package. *He's changed.* He's still wearing his perfect fit boot-cut jeans that hang *oh so low* off his waist, but now in a black fitted T that shows off his lean chiseled abs, and a black leather bomber jacket with an *AX* on the lower right-hand corner of the zipper.

Holy crap! He's wearing Armani! Thanks to Mandy I know what that looks like.

He pulls out a five-dollar bill and puts it down next to his cup and begins to walk away.

"Hey...don't you want your change?"

"The barista service was excellent." He says winking at me.

"I hope to see you tomorrow evening."

"Be prepared. My skills are pretty awesome." I say mockingly with a smile.

He gives me one last devious smirk, turns, and leaves.

Holy shit! That look, that sexy debonair look. My stomach flutters and my limbs start to tingle. A huge grin sweeps across my face and I'm already anxious for tomorrow.

I shake my head knowing I succumbed to *Hotties* charm. I should know better. He's totally out of my league.

My experience with "men" is equal to well "none". In high school I dated guys who were barely hitting puberty and were immature morons. Their jockstrap and Xbox got more attention than I did. I've never had anything in common with guys my age.

I spent more time rolling my eyes, annoyed by their adolescence than anything. I wouldn't even know how to act with someone like Alex.

I walk around the counter and head over to the door. Looking out into the darkness, I wish Alex hadn't left. But it's not like I could ask a total stranger to sit here and wait to walk me home after I lock up anyway. What is there to be afraid of so close to campus anyway? I lock the door and turn off the outdoor light. Suddenly feeling the depth of my loneliness.

I wipe down the bistro tables, the bar counter, and the machines.

Clean out the industrial coffee pots and the rest of the dishes. Sweep the floor and mop.

***

It's 11:45 p.m. and I'm exhausted. Mr. T told me to leave the register as is and with that thought I go to his office and grab my bag and the shop keys.

Ready to leave I head for the back door. I come out, close it, and lock it tight. When I turn around, I realize I'm in the back alley of Mochas. I take in a deep breath and look around nervously.

Just walk around the corner and you are home free.

The campus is just a few blocks away. I start to walk and walk fast. I suddenly have that eerie feeling again. The one I had outside of Mandy's house. The feeling of being watched, and now I'm starting to panic. I start to pick up speed and know that I am only seconds away from the openness. I look back consciously believing there's someone behind me. That's when I begin to run.

I'm running so fast that I'm on campus ground in less than a minute. I feel safer already. Though, that feeling is still there, and my hands begin to sweat and heat from anxiety. I look back once more and see nothing.

When I turn around my heart jumps to my throat and I scream!

"BIANCA!! What the hell?! You can't just jump out and scare people like that!" I scold her.

Bent over, resting my sweaty hands on my knees, trying to calm my rapid heart and heated body, I feel as if I'm going to pass out.

Bianca of course is laughing hysterically.

"I'm...so...sorry." she says clutching her stomach.

"I saw the opportunity and I took it. You looked like you were already scared. How could I not?"

Bitch! I just want to hit her.

"You scared the shit out of me! Look at me! I'm still shaking! I can't believe you did that to me." I say trembling and infuriated.

My palms feel like they are on fire and sweat beads down my forehead from the nervous heat rushing through my body.

"Okay...okay. Calm down. I shouldn't have done that. I'm really sorry." She says with a sincere smile and a small snicker.

"What were you running from anyways? You looked like something was chasing you." She says looking around puzzled.

"It was nothing. I was just trying to get back to the dorm. It's late and I'm tired."

I look around still feeling paranoid. I honestly don't know what I was running from.

"Let's just go." I say agitated.

I breathe heavily in and out trying to calm myself. Then I remember what time it is and I look at her in confusion.

"Wait. Where were you? It's almost midnight."

"Oh...nowhere, just in the campus cruiser with Josh." She says all nonchalant.

"What? Campus Security Guard Josh?"

"He IS an actual Police Officer. He's not a fake Cop you know." Now I'm the one being scolded.

"Besides...he's really hot in that uniform."

"And what were you doing with "Police Officer" Josh?" I say with an eyebrow raised in suspicion.

"Oh you know...he was just showing me his stick...in the back seat of the Cruiser." She says with a devious and sexy look.

"Oh...my God." I say rolling my eyes.

"I know right. Who knew I was such a slut."

We both giggle and I shove Bianca with my shoulder.

"You just met Josh a week ago and you're already getting laid."

"Oh honey...I got laid the first night we met."

"That's got to be some sort of record here at Duke. I think most guys would be jealous of your talent."

We giggle again. I would have never guessed her to be so promiscuous, but I have no ill judgment. I would do it too if I were as out-going as her.

Bianca is prancing around me like a little school girl and I can't help but laugh and smile at her giddiness.

"Yup! You're a slut!" I say laughing.

She smiles and shrugs her shoulders not even caring. As we walk to the East dorm hall Bianca gives me the scoop on her night, going into every detail of her sexual escapade and I of course listen intently, overwhelmed with curiosity.

***

BACK IN THE ROOM with Bianca sound asleep, I lay in bed and think of Alex. The grin across my face has been glued to me for the past half hour. I lay awake unable to sleep when all I see when I close my eyes is his gorgeous blues. I've never had the giddy, butterflies in the stomach feeling about a guy before. I almost want to squeal from the excitement I feel. I shake my head at how Alex a.k.a. *Mr. Hottie* has me melting in the palm of his hand right now. I don't even know anything about him except that he's obviously wealthy, totally freaking hot, and likes having decaf coffee at 11:00 o'clock at night. *Weird.* I didn't even think to ask why he was out so late.

After daydreaming a little more, exhaustion finally hits me. As much as I want to lay awake and think about Alex's mesmerizing eyes and sexy smile, my eyelids begin to droop. I gladly give into the tired feeling and close my eyes, hoping the vision of Alex will lead me to dream of him.

Eleven

I see it so clear, the bright white light ahead. It's almost blinding. I'm running towards it wanting to see where it leads. Then I see a figure come into the light. As I strain for a closer look, I see it's a woman, a woman I recognize. It can't be. I see her and I'm ready to leap at her.

She stands there, holding her arms out for me, smiling. She looks so beautiful. Her thin and brittle body draped in a beautiful white gown...her long auburn hair lying wavy along her shoulders...her chocolate brown eyes bold and bright.

She's waiting to embrace me. I call out to her. "Mom!" I can't believe it's her. I take off faster towards her, ready to leap into her arms and hold her tight but as much as I run I'm still so far away. She's calling me and her voice makes me speed up.

What is she looking at though? Why is she looking behind me? Her blissfulness has suddenly tured to terror. She sees something behind me. She shouts at me to hurry. I'm afraid now, afraid to look back, to see what she sees.

I run faster but I'm not moving. I'm in a tunnel shrouded with trees and the light at the end seems to stretch. "Mom! Please! Help me!" I cry out reaching for her. I see tears fall from her cheek. She shakes her head and drops her hands as if there's no hope.

I don't understand. Why won't she come to me? My eyes begin to flood knowing she's letting me go.

She gives me a sorrowful pained look and turns away. My heart feels wounded and faint, and I begin to slow down, not caring anymore for what awaits me.

I close my eyes and come to a stop. I want to fall to the floor and curl in a ball, but I suddenly realize I'm not alone.

I slowly turn around to face whatever horror lies behind me. When I open my eyes, the tunnel of light around me fades with only a light surrounding my body. But soon that too begins to fade, clouded by a dark mist. I take in a deep breath... and darkness devours me.

"MIA! Hello! Are you going to get the alarm? It's been going off for the past ten minutes!" Bianca shouts frustrated from underneath her duvet cover.

I quickly open my eyes and I'm relieved to see the popcorn ceiling of my dorm room. It's barely sunrise and I'm grateful to see a bit of light peeking through the blinds. *It was just a dream.*

I reach over and hit my alarm off.

"Sorry. I didn't even hear it. I guess I was really out." I say apologetically.

"Ugh...I don't want to get up. Why did we stay up so late?" Bianca moans.

"Because you couldn't stop talking about how big of a tramp you are." We both giggle.

As my smile fades, I lay there, thinking about my nightmare, about seeing my mom. I swallow hard trying to hold back the tears from forming. *What did it mean?*

I sit up and throw my legs over the side of the bed and let them hang, still so tired.

Once again, my body feels like it's on fire and I'm drenched in sweat.

Gross. I need a cold shower.

I can't let the dream bother me. That's all it was. A bad dream. I finally jump off the bed and stretch, trying to wake up. I grab my iPhone, hit the Pandora app, set it to *Bush*, and put it on the speaker doc.

"Time to get up!" I shout.

"No...I don't want to." Bianca wines, still hiding under her duvet.

"I'll drag you out of there." I say laughing.

"Just 20 more minutes." She says sleepily.

I run over to her bed and plop down bouncing over and over.

"It's time to get up...it's time to get up...it's time to get up for the morning." I sing.

Bianca laughs and finally throws the blanket off her head.

"Wow! Someone forgot to take off their mascara last night. You look like a raccoon." I say laughing.

"Ha...ha! Very funny. I was too tired." she says groggily.

"Well...I'm up and I'm going to hit the shower."

"Yeah...you need it. Geeze Mia. You look like you went into the shower with your clothes on. Gross."

"Yeah, I don't know what's going on with me. Lately I've been waking up drenched and feeling like my body just came out of the furnace."

"Well get your butt to the shower, you disgusting mop you." She laughs.

"Yeah...yeah...I'm going."

"K...I'll be there in a few." Bianca says throwing her duvet back over her head.

I walk over to the wardrobe closet, pull out a towel and my shower caddy, put on my flip flops, and walk out the door.

The hallways are still dark and dim as usual at 7:00 a.m. Most of the students sleep in, only waking ten minutes before their first class begins and sometimes go in their PJ's.

Still sleepy and yawning, I make my way to the shower room. As soon as I walk in, the censored lights flick on. I look down to the end of the long row of showers and contemplate whether I want to go ahead and take the large handicap shower at the very end or just the regular small one. I shrug my shoulders and go for the big one. There are at least twenty other showers and everyone's still asleep, so no one will care if I take it.

I step in and close the shower curtain. I hang my caddy on the wall hook, throw my towel over the rod, and begin stripping off my clothes.

Standing there naked I'm suddenly halted by the sound of footsteps. I quietly wait a minute questioning who it could be. The steps are slow, heavy and loud.

"Bianca? Is that you?" I shout.

I hear no response and the footsteps have paused. I wait a minute to see if I hear anything, and I hear nothing. Uncertain, I grab my towel and wrap it around my body.

I peek out the side of the shower curtain and look down the long row of empty showers. I don't see or hear a thing. Then...the lights go out.

My heart begins to race. I'm nervous and scared. That heated feeling of what I think is anxiety begins to overtake my body again.

I can still see through the dim shower room but I'm frozen where I stand. Still peering out and seeing nothing, I slowly pull back the curtain, step out, and wave my arms around towards the ceiling trying to trigger the censor.

Nothing happens. *Shit!*

Knowing I'm going to have to do something besides stand here waiting, I start to walk towards the exit. The curtains to each of the showers are pulled back leaving it easy for me to see into them.

I slowly and cautiously walk by each one. Towards the middle of the row, I see one shower curtain closed.

I'm frozen again, wondering whether I should just run past it to the door, or if I should pull it back to see if there's someone in there playing games with me.

Quit being a coward!

Angry with my subconscious, I walk up to the curtain and quickly pull it back. *Nothing.* I sigh in relief and laugh at myself, feeling silly.

Suddenly I jump from the sound of a voice.

"Why are the lights off?" Bianca asks standing by the door staring at me.

"Shit! You scared me...again." I stand there panting and holding my chest.

"Hmm...I seem to be pretty good at that." She says smiling at me.

"They were on for a few minutes and then went off. I can't seem to get them back on."

As soon as Bianca walks through the doorway the lights come on.

"Well...they seem to be working just fine now." She says still sleepy.

Bianca walks to the first shower stall and turns it on.

I look at her up and down seeing that she's wrapped in a towel and wearing flip flops. When she walked by me, I didn't hear the same sound as earlier.

Who was in here?

"You okay? You look lost." She says looking at me with her brow raised.

"I'm fine. I guess I'm still asleep."

Feeling like an idiot I walk back down to the end of the row, jump back into the handicap shower stall, and close the curtain.

I turn on the water, throw my towel back over the rod, and walk under. Washing my hair, I start to think I'm going crazy.

Did I really hear footsteps or was it just my mind playing tricks on me?

I think about all the things I've been through and wonder if maybe I need therapy. I feel like everything from my past is finally catching up to me.

Sheriff Daniels tried to get me to see our local counselor, but I refused. Even though patient confidentiality should protect me, the town would somehow know everything about my utterly irrational psychosis. Maybe I just need to admit I experienced something very traumatic in my life and see a therapist.

I rinse out my hair, wash my body, and relax under the warmth of the water. I want to think about something else besides how much therapy I need.

I smile instantly knowing what I can think about. *Alex.* Grinning I close my eyes and I let my imagination take over:

Alex opens the shower curtain and steps in with his bare sculpted body, gazing into my eyes with lust and determination. He closes in, his stature hovering over me as his hand gently brushes against my cheek.

I reach for his forearms and slowly pull him into me, feeling his length harden between my legs. My body shudders and pants as he lays kisses along my neck line. He wraps his muscular arms around me, pulling me in closer.

The warmth of his body and the water embraces me, and I melt. Our hands explore one another's body seeking the touch and feel of every detail. His hand tangles in my hair and pulls my head back to gaze into his eyes.

When my eyes meet his with the same want, he delivers me a hard, sensuous, delicious kiss. Our mouths open wide allowing our tongues to slowly intertwine with rhythm while his hands massage and caress...

"Mia! Are you done? You've been in there for a while."

I jump, winded and alarmed by the interruption.

"Uhm...yeah. Be out in a minute." I shout trying to catch my breath.

Twelve

Lucius walks in to the dining room and takes a seat. He stretches his legs up onto the table and leans back with his hands behind his head. He has this look of pure pleasure written across his face by the look of his wide grin.

"What are you so happy about?" I ask.

"I just received word that Brutus returned to The Council to deliver your message. I also heard that Marcus was very displeased with Brutus, so much so, that he was punished by Marcus in front of the Council. Apparently, it was quite a gruesome scene. I'm only disappointed I was not there to see it."

I shake my head and continue to read.

"So brother, tell me all about your evening with our dear Mia."

"There's nothing to be said. We briefly spoke. I made sure she was safe and alone in the building. That's all." I say not bothered by his intrusive questioning.

"I see. And will you be having more of these brief conservations with our dear Mia?"

I don't know why he keeps calling her *our* Mia but it's beginning to agitate me.

"I would imagine so. I think there's a great benefit to having a close eye on her." I say nonchalantly.

"Is that so? The only benefit brother?"

Flustered I put my book down

"Oh do come out with it. What is it you wish to ask?"

"I simply wish to know, whether I might have the opportunity to chat with Mia myself. Maybe I want to ensure her safety in close quarters as well."

I stand raged.

Lucius laughs and puts his hands up in surrender.

"Well, now isn't this interesting. You care for her quite deeply. The funny thing is you've been denying yourself the truth."

Lucius did that on purpose to get a reaction out of me and I think it surprised us both, well, at least it surprised me.

"Yes. I do care for her. I can't quite understand it. I've never felt this way before." Lucius tilts his head as if he wants to correct me.

"I cared for Genevieve but in a different way. Not like this brother. I want to be near her all the time. I crave her presence. I crave...her."

I walk up to the fireplace, losing my thoughts as I stare at the burning ambers.

I don't know what's come over me. We've barely interacted, but there's an electrifying connection between us.

Lucius stands and makes his way over to me.

"Bloody hell. You've got it bad brother. I must say it's quite amusing to see you so distressed over a woman this way." He chuckles.

"Always in control. But you can't control when love happens. I know this well." Lucius looks away, hiding his solemnness no less, over his beloved. I know he thinks of her often.

But love? I've felt forms of it before but not for a woman in this manner.

I remember loving my mother, of course it was different. But the last time I remember a true form of love was with her, my mother Amara.

My mother was the most amazing woman I've ever known. When my father died from an infected war wound, she was left to care for me on her own.

I remember every detail of her. Her long dark hair, black as a raven. Her pale skin aged and brittle by hard labor and the sun. Her soul, however, kept her young. The bright light inside her gave her youth. That and her bright blue eyes. As blue as the sea.

I will never forget how the smell of her mint palm oil skin and how her hair smelled of marjoram. Cleanliness was very important to my mother. Even though we didn't have much, she made sure we were clean for only slaves had poor hygiene.

We lived in a small village 100 miles outside of Rome. My mother did what she could for money. She was quite talented really. She hemmed legionnaire uniforms, repaired footwear, and cooked meals for soldiers coming through town, returning home from battle.

I helped her as much as I could, for I was only twelve at the time. I ran errands for the townsfolks by retrieving water from the river, fishing and hunting animals for the women whose husbands were away at post. It was just she and I for some time.

Lucius was also an only child, though his upbringing was far different than mine. His mother was one of many prostitutes in the village. She earned coin the only way she knew how. Lucius never knew his father for there was no way to really know. Even though Lucius was a child of circumstance, he was unwelcome by many. A bastard child.

Even though they were treated poorly by the village, my mother did not have an unkind bone in her body and was the only person that spoke kindly to Lucius and his mother Alexia. My mother knew Alexia cared for Lucius, and that unfortunate circumstances led her to her position. She was raped at a very young age and thrown out by her own parents. Alexia turned to the only way to earn coin when you are a female with nothing.

Lucius was Alexia's first born and the only child that survived past birth. Lucius had six other brothers and sisters that did not survive. We may not have been born as brothers, but we were just as inseparable.

Many nights Lucius stayed with my mother and I when Alexia had men over for the night. Most of the time, Army soldiers passing through were her biggest patrons. Lucius's presence was an unwelcome interference in their eyes.

Alexia wanted Lucius safe so she would pay my mother to look after Lucius, but my mother would never accept her coin. She loved Lucius as if he were her own.

When we were 14 years of age, Lucius and I were coming back from a hunting trip and saw his mother Alexia arguing with a Captain who refused to pay her. He, without remorse, plunged his sword straight through her.

We ran to Alexia to help her, but she was already dead. Before either of us could do anything stupid, Hektor, our village blacksmith, grabbed a hold of us. My mother saw what happened and ran over to help Hektor keep us under control.

Lucius was filled with rage and pain and was ready to attack. Had Hektor not held onto Lucius, he would have met his mother in the afterlife. There was no consideration from the Roman Army for they were superior over Rome's citizens.

I will never forget the sobs and screams from Lucius. It was one of the most painful memories I have. His mother loved him dearly, and he loved her.

It took many months before Lucius was any resemblance of his normal self. Hektor pressured his recovery with fighting lessons. Even when his days seemed unbearable, Hektor never allowed Lucius to sulk.

Hektor became our saving grace. He taught Lucius and I to grapple and wield various weapons, including a sword and spear. Hektor was a Battalion leader when he served before being discharged for an injury. He passed on his knowledge of warfare knowing we would likely join the very military we hated.

When we turned 17, we were recruited to join the Roman Army, and by the grace of Gods, we quickly moved up in rank. We were faster and more efficient than any Hoplite foot soldier. With our knowledge of military tactics, Lucius and I became Captains then Battalion Leaders.

After spending eight years in battle after battle, Lucius and I finally had the chance to briefly come home. It was then that we learned my mother was dead. She was pillaged by vagabonds passing through the village. Hektor tried to save her, but there were too many men and he too was killed. We were devastated. The remorse we both felt for leaving them was agonizing.

What I remember clearly about love, is that loving someone and then losing them is an unbearable pain.

I care for Mia more than I ever thought I could. I may even love her, but I know that I must tread carefully. Our worlds collide for a different reason. I'm meant to safeguard her from those who wish to harm her.

If something terrible happens to Mia, I don't think I will be able to survive it. If *the Council* comes for her again, I'll be ready.

Thirteen

My classes have been beyond boring. All I can do is think about Alex, so anxious to see him again, to look deep into his radiant blue eyes, and see that sexy ass grin.

As I make my way up to the back of my *Creative Writing* class, taught by my Lit Professor, I see the seat Alex sat in and I smile at the memory. As I sit, I'm abruptly startled by the presence of someone who sits down right next to me.

"Hi...." he says.

"Hi..." I reply without even looking at my neighbor.

I pay no attention to him as I know it's not Alex. I'm a little distraught and over territorial at the moment, unsure why he decided to sit right next to "me". I guess I'm just feeling a little defensive, thinking that seat is indefinitely Alex's. I'm not sure why when he's not even a student. He was just observing my Literature class yesterday.

Pouting, I pull out my book and notepad and prepare for lecture. As the Professor goes on about famous novelists and play writing, I'm gently nudged.

"Sorry to bug...but do you have an extra pen. Mine's not working. I guess that's what I get for buying cheap pens."

I look up at my neighbor and I'm instantly speechless. I'm blindsided by two wide, honey hazel eyes. I bite my lower lip to shut my shocked and gaping mouth.

"Uhm...sure." I shyly reply and hand over a pen.

"Thanks. I appreciate it." He says taking it and then turns to face forward.

I however, can't take my eyes off him. He's got that all American, small town, look. He's wearing a faded American Eagle long sleeve T-shirt, warn out low rise boot-cut jeans, and brown leather flip-flops. *Flip-flops when it's winter here.*

His skin is a beautiful golden tan that matches his shaggy but groomed, sun-kissed blond hair. I assume he must come from a sunny state because North Carolina winter wouldn't give anyone that great tan. He resembles Paul Walker in so many ways. *Yum.*

He looks over at me, gazing, and I automatically smile. Then of course I flush and look down shy. Once again, I find myself mesmerized by a hot guy in class instead of listening to the Professors lecture.

What is it with this room?

Even though he's quite the catch, I can't help but think about Alex, wondering if he'll make it to Mocha's tonight or if I'm a fool for thinking he will keep his word. After all, he is a rich *Hottie* who could get anyone he wanted. Why on earth would he want some college student who works at a coffee shop? I shake my head at how naive I am, thinking that Alex, a.k.a. *Mr. Hottie* is coming to see "me".

Stupid lust.

I should just get over him and get my head wrapped around school. I finally convince myself to focus on the Professors lecture and I begin taking notes.

Class dismisses early and with a writing assignment. I grab my bag and throw everything in, exhausted from the long and dull day. I get up and walk down the stairs to the door, standing behind a crowd of students trying to leave class.

I turn around to the sound of mumbled voices and see *Hazel Eyes* talking to the Professor. *Totally cute.* As I watch them chit chat, he turns my way and smiles at me. Ugh...caught again! I immediately face forward and rush through the crowd feeling embarrassed.

I still have a couple of hours before my shift begins so I decide to head to the Perkins/Bockston library to get a head start on my assignment.

I could easily get what I need off the web, but I love being in a big library, surrounded by history, fantasy, quotes of great authors...and the smell of old dingy paper and beaten down hard covers.

It makes me think about my parents. That old dingy smell consumed their study. Sometimes I just want a sweet reminder of what home felt like during the best of times. Besides, the Perkins/Bockston library is pretty impressive. I love getting lost in it.

***

This library...is huge!! Four stories and two sublevel basements packed with books galore. I'm still amazed each time I'm here by how enormous it is. I'm so ready to be submerged in the amazing collection of books.

I walk over to the reference and research area of the first floor and look up T.S. Eliot. I find a list of his poems and plays, and know which one I want to write a critical analysis essay on. *Murder in the Cathedral.* It's an awesome play by Eliot. It's written in verse over the assassination of Archbishop Thomas Becket in 1170. Eliot's writing is based on the eye witness of a Clerk named Edward Grim. I interpret it as Grim's protest against certain religious aspects of the Christian Church. I love this play because it has specific meaning to me.

I've never really been a Church goer, mainly because of Church politics. I find Church organizations to be contradictory. It doesn't mean I don't believe in God, or maybe I don't know, I just don't feel comfortable with someone lecturing me on "how" I should believe in God or Gods, especially when it's the rule makers who are the biggest rule breakers.

Now that I've found where Eliot's books are located, I head to the elevators to retrieve a copy. Basement, sub-level 2.

When the doors open, the old dingy smell surrounds me, and I immediately feel at peace. It's quiet, enclosed and just like home.

I'm finally alone with my favorite Authors: T.S. *Eliot, Jane Austen, Charles Dickens, Thomas Hardy, Emily Bronte*...they're all here to comfort me with love, drama, adventure and wonder.

Making my way through the aisles, I find that I really am alone, which actually doesn't bother me. I would rather tussle through the tower of books by myself and daydream away.

I find most of Eliot's works and pull out *Murder in the Cathedral*. I go to one of the study areas, sit down, take out my notepad and pen, and begin taking notes. No real need to borrow it since I've read it a dozen times. I just need reference pages and quotes.

As I get lost in the theatrical melancholy of the verses, I feel a presence in front of me. I slowly look up and jump when I see him, *Hazel Eyes*.

"I'm so sorry. I didn't mean to scare you. I said hello but I think you were pretty absorbed by your book." he says apologetically.

"It's okay...I just thought I was alone down here."

"I think you are." he says looking around.

"I just came down to look for a book. And here I thought "I" was going to be the only one down here. No one really comes to libraries anymore."

"I know...sort of sad." I say looking around depressed.

"The web or Amazon are the preferred method these days. Don't get me wrong, I love my kindle, but I love the feel of an old hard cover book more."

"Yeah...me too. My Granddad had a huge collection of books and he use to sit me on his lap and read me a book for hours. The smell of old books remind me of him."

I smile at him for the similar appreciation of books and his care-free thought of someone so close.

"I'm sorry, I should introduce myself. I'm Noah." He says sweetly, holding out his hand.

"Nice to meet you Noah. I'm Mia."

I shake his hand and feel comforted by the warmth of his hand.

"You know. I don't think I've ever seen you in Creative Writing class before." I say.

Noah smiles.

"Yeah...I usually sit in the middle of the class but all last semester, the Professors speech was getting drowned out by two girls that sat next to me. They liked to gossip a lot. So, I thought I would try higher grounds."

"Got it. I'm surprised you've managed all this time." I tease.

"So...what are you looking for?" I ask.

"*The Village Coquettes* by *Dickens*. It's a pretty interesting assign-ment, to do an analytical essay on short a play. I'm a fan of *Dickens* so I thought I would find one of his very few plays to write about. You?"

"*T.S. Eliot's, Murder in the Cathedral*. It's one of my favorite plays." I say shyly, not wanting to go into detail why.

"I think I've seen the movie. If it's by Eliot, I'm sure it's great." He says standing there putting his hands in his pocket.

"So...what are you majoring in?" he asks.

"Uhm...I'm not really sure yet. I've sort of thought about major-ing in Literature or who knows, creative writing."

"Then this assignment must be exciting for you." he says with a big bright smile.

"I guess you could say that. It all depends on the content." I say playfully.

"How about yourself?" I ask.

"I was actually thinking about Journalism."

"Interesting. So am I going to see you on the 6 o'clock news in a year?" I say smirking.

"No...that won't be me. I'm more of the behind the scenes kinda guy. More like newspaper and magazine articles."

"That's great." I say approvingly.

"Do you mind having company? I was gonna grab my book and sit with you. That's if you don't mind?" He says, gazing down at me.

How could I mind when he asks with those beautiful hazel eyes and sweet smile. Of course I don't mind.

"No...not at all. Please feel free."

Yup...there goes getting any work done. I'm pretty sure I'm going to be distracted the entire time I'm here. *Oh well.* It's a nice distraction.

"Cool. I'm just gonna grab my book. I'll be right back."

I watch Noah walk away to the middle aisle to look through the shelves. As he reaches up at the top shelf, his muscular arms flex from forearm to bicep tightening his shirt sleeves. Even in the dim light of this basement I can see the sheen of his blond hair on the golden tanned skin of his neck. I also realize how tall he really is. He has to be over six foot. Lean and broad shouldered, like an Olympic swimmers build. I'm beginning to daydream about what's underneath the t-shirt.

I flinch when I see him turn my way. Trying to refocus and act as if I'm reading, I look down and turn the page.

Noah takes a seat across from me. We look at one another for a moment...then look down at our books. I suddenly feel hot and fidgety. I started a fire when I let my thoughts wander over his body. *Ugh...focus!*

Fourteen

We've been sitting quietly for the past hour reading our books and taking notes. I look up at him every now and then to see what he's doing, catching him through my peripheral vision doing the same. Finally, Noah breaks the silence.

"So...where are you from?" he says sitting back against his seat.

"A small town out of Oregon called Silverton. You?" I say, smiling at his smirk.

"Born and raised in Justin, Texas. It's sort of small town too but we're not too far from the city." He says crossing his arms.

"My parents own a horse ranch there." He says and smiles.

I smile in return.

"What do your parents do?"

The question pierces me, and my face goes grim. I look down unsure how to answer that question. Do I really want to tell a total stranger about my parents and how they were murdered? Or do I want to hide it by lying and leave the pity for someone else? I pick the lesser of two evils.

"They're Historians for the University of Cambridge but work from home." I say with less enthusiasm.

"Wow. That's pretty impressive. I'm surprised you aren't at Cambridge. Wouldn't you get a discount on tuition or something?"

"Uhm yeah... I actually would. Pretty much a free ride. I just didn't want to leave...the U.S. I luckily received a few scholarships and three years are paid in full. I've applied for a few more for next year." I smile weakly.

"That's great! I applied for a few as well but I was only able to get my first two years paid for. Duke is pretty expensive. My parents joke around all the time, telling me how they're gonna have to sell the ranch and their organs to pay for school." He says laughing.

"There are hundreds, maybe even thousands of scholarships out there that no one even knows about. I Googled scholarships and applied for over fifty. I was approved by almost every single one. They're pretty easy to apply for. I'm sure you'll get your free ride." I smile hesitantly thinking about how that came out.

We sit there looking at one another not knowing what else to say. Noah gives me this cute smirk and I give him a quick smile before looking down, shy and full of butterflies.

"Hey...do you have any plans for dinner? I hear there's a great pizza joint close to the campus and I was wondering if you might join me...and maybe we can throw in some writing time."

As he leans in waiting for my answer, I'm lost in the combination of colors. The mixture of greens and golds, swirling in perfection around his irises. The florescent light magnifies the warmth of his eyes and brightens like a gorgeous sunrise. Still lost in his eyes I finally answer.

"Okay...Oh wait! I forgot. I have to work tonight."

Shit! Realizing how much time has passed, I jump in my seat. I dig in my bag for my phone in search for the time.

"Crap! I'm so sorry. I have to go. I got to get back to the dorm and get ready for my shift. I would love to have pizza with you another time though?"

"Sure. We have all semester." he says jokingly and smiles.

Gathering my things, I hurriedly stand and grab the book to put it up. Noah follows me with his book as well. I head for the aisle where I found my book and I reach up to slip it in its slot. Struggling, Noah comes up behind me and gently takes it from my hand and slides it in between two books on the top shelf. I turn around and he's hovering at least a foot over me, smiling down at me, making me feel week in the knees by his proximity.

"Thanks." I say staring into his eyes.

He sweetly smiles. "No problem."

I struggle to part our gaze but finally manage to look away. I start to walk towards the elevator and Noah's there to push the button for me. We stand there staring at the elevator doors fidgeting.

"So ...where do you work?"

"A coffee shop called Mocha's, just off campus grounds."

"I've seen that place. Good to know." He says smirking.

When the doors open, I step in and turn to face him.

"I guess I'll see you around."

"Yeah...see ya."

He stands there looking at me, wanting to say more but doesn't. I gaze at him hoping he does, and then the doors close. I sigh and push the level 1 button, fanning myself, still feeling heated from our closeness. A hot and sexy guy just asked me out on a date and I had to say no. *What the fudge?! Ugh!* Well, at least I'll see him in couple of days. How did I get so lucky to have met two hot guys within two days? Whatever worlds have collided to make this happen, I'm happy for the momentary satisfaction.

***

Work has been pretty slow. We've only had a dozen customers since I started my shift at six. No one has ordered anything too extravagant either, so no need to practice my Barista skills. Smiling at how that sounds I can only think of one thing.

As I look around and see a nearly empty shop, I sigh from disappointment. It's almost ten and no sign of Alex. I should have known he wasn't going to show. Flirting and wooing me just because he can. I was an idiot to think he would actually come. He's probably not even from around here and went back to the lands of the wealthy.

Stupid...I don't even know the guy! Why can't I get him out of my mind? I was so anxious and excited to see him today. Well...there goes that.

"Mia...I'm leaving now. You good to close again?" says Mr. T.

"Sure. No problem."

"I can't tell you how much we appreciate your help. Our daughter was able to help us here and there, but she has been really busy with school. I'm sure you'll eventually meet her. Oh...and I was thinking next week I could just leave for the day once you start your shift. You have already done so well within the past two days. It will also help me and my wife have time to run errands at home."

"That's totally fine. I think I'll be able to manage by then. Go home and get some rest."

"Okay. See you tomorrow Mia."

"Bye."

After Mr. T leaves I run to the back office and get my bag. I figure I can get some work done since we're so slow. I grab it and run back up to the front and pull out my Mac and set it on the bar counter. I turn on the computer and pull up a new doc and begin typing.

I type away not thinking about anything but getting my assignment done. Before I know it, it's already closing time and the shop is empty. I walk around the counter up to the front door to turn off the light and lock up. As I lock the door and look out into the night, I feel another pain of disappointment. There's a part of me that's hoping Alex will still show. Knowing he's not going to, I walk away and begin cleaning up.

Locking up the back door I get that feeling again, like I'm being watched. I close my eyes, upset with myself for letting my scared little subconscious get to me again. When I open them, I put on a strong front and begin to walk with my head held high. I should probably go ahead and see a therapist. Its times like this that I know I should seek help. I was never scared of anything before the murder. I know it's the memory of that night that will forever have me fearful.

Once I get around the corner, I see campus ground and I feel relieved. I step onto the campus sidewalk that's hidden under the dark hollow trees. I walk on trying not to think about how the pathway looks, but then I hear footsteps somewhere behind me.

I walk faster. Then I speed my step and the footsteps behind me begin to close in on me. Now I'm really scared. My body begins to heat and shake, and I feel this overwhelming sensation like I'm losing control. *Please not an anxiety attack.*

It's late and I'm alone in the night. Just as I'm about to take off running to save myself from passing out, I hear him.

"Mia!" I turn around, and I'm stunned when I see him only a few feet behind me.

"Alex?"

Fifteen

"I'm sorry Mia. I hope I didn't frighten you."

"Frighten me? Alex it's almost midnight. Of course you frightened me!" I say agitated.

How dare he show up this late after I waited all night for him.

"I'm very sorry. I tried to catch you before you closed but I had business to attend to and it took a little longer than I expected." He says sincerely.

I stare at him, angry, not saying a thing.

"I understand if you're upset with me. Again...my sincerest apologies."

I'm still glaring at him not wanting to say a word. Allowing time for my body to settle down.

"Mia. Please forgive me." He says with a sorrowful and pitiful look.

"Stop. No more apologies. It was no big deal. I honestly forgot about you coming anyway." I say nonchalantly.

Yeah right! Liar!

"Look, it's late. I'm on my way back to the dorm. Maybe we can catch up another time."

Standing there pouting, all I can really focus on is those beautiful eyes. I could stand here all night looking at the beautiful glowing sapphires.

"May I walk you?"

I nod. "Sure."

We walk in silence, both unsure what to say. This evening didn't exactly turn out the way I expected. I was hoping we would have another flirt session in the shop so I could get to know him better.

I know the look of frustration is written across my face. Looking over at him, worried that he'll see my expression, I see he has the same look across his face.

I laugh to myself thinking about how we must look together, walking in the dark, distraught and grim.

"So why is it that a business entrepreneur is out so late?"

He looks at me and smiles delighted by the sudden change in our mood.

"A lot of my business is discussed over late...dinners... and sometimes we go for...drinks afterwards." A broad smirk gleams across his face like I'm missing some inside joke.

"I see."

"So, is this a nightly routine? If so, you must not get a lot of sleep."

"Lately...yes. Either way, I don't sleep much." He says.

"Are you in Durham only for business or for pleasure?"

I see that sexy smirk on him again.

"I hope both." He says looking devious.

Oh crap! I didn't think about how that would come out.

"I'm mainly here for business. I'm staying in a Condo I just purchased not too far from here."

"Oh...so how long are you planning on staying around Durham? I figured you would rent a spot if you aren't staying long."

"For a while. I think my business here might take longer than expected. I actually like it here a lot. The Condo was selling for a great price since it needed a lot of work done." He says charmingly.

We continue to circle the campus talking about his business and the places he's been, which is almost everywhere in the world. London, Japan, Greece, and his favorite, Rome. Then we talk about my classes, my possible major and the atmosphere of the Campus. He listens intently and asks a few questions here and there, giving me that sexy smirk in between.

It still boggles my mind that he's even here with me. I just can't imagine what it is about me that he's so interested in. He could have any New York style housewife/model at his side right now.

Contemplating what it could be, my face gives me away.

"What are you thinking about? You seem to be concentrating pretty hard." He says smiling, intrigued.

We stop in our footing and I face him, wanting to see the truth in him.

"I guess...I'm just wondering why you're here with me right now."

His smile turns flat.

"I'm afraid I don't understand."

"Well...you seem like a great guy who's well educated and wealthy, and I'm an average Jane college student who served you coffee late one night. I'm just curious to know what made you come back."

"I haven't quite analyzed it as you have. For now, I see it as I met a beautiful girl who's charmed me. Do you always ask why someone is interested in you? I would think it's quite clear why I'm interested." He gazes down deep into my eyes, giving me that weak feeling in my knees...as tender chills, slowly creeps up my body.

"No...not really."

He has me in in his trance again. All I can think about is how he thinks I'm beautiful.

Breathe.

My eyes are locked onto his. I'm quietly panting, and my heart is jumping in hoops. I finally look down, finding relief from the overwhelming feeling he's given me.

He brings his hand up, as if he's going to touch me, but hesitates. He clenches his fist and swallows. H releases his fist and brushes his hands against my cheek. I close my eyes letting the sensation of his touch consume me.

He pulls me closer to him and gently lifts my chin, urging me to look at him. I open my eyes and he's staring at me with a look of pain. I don't know what to make of it.

My eyes search for understanding and before I can pull from his hold, he softly kisses me. I close my eyes again as the warmth of his smooth plush lips against mine sends shivers down my spine. My legs are tingling, and my arms go limp. Then I feel a rush of heat run up through my body.

He pulls back slowly, leaving me standing there with my eyes still closed. I finally open them and see he's struggling, tightening his jaw as if he's restraining himself. He wants more. So do I.

I'm unaware of my surroundings, still lost in a dream from that gentle, amazing, kiss.

"Is this your dorm?" he says tenderly brushing my cheek again.

I look around still dazed and confused, but recognize my dorm building.

"Uhm...Yes." I shake myself from my daze and come to.

"Do you want to walk me up?" I ask shyly.

"It would be my pleasure." He says moving my hair over my shoulder.

We walk in, both smiling and pleased with what just happened. We take the stairs to the second level and walk down the hallway. Only a few doors down from my room, I look back to see if Alex is following me and see him standing there, hands at his side fisted.

He looks like he senses something. I look around trying to figure out what he sees or feels.

"Alex...are you okay?" I ask wearily.

"Yes...sorry. I thought I...heard something."

"Oh...what did you hear?"

"It was nothing. It's very late. You should get inside your room." He says with his brows furrowed.

"Is something wrong?"

He suddenly realizes how he must have come across and ...He walks up to me and grabs my hand. He pulls it up to his mouth and kisses it.

"Of course not. I just know that I'm keeping you from getting your rest. I'm sure you have class in the morning, and I don't want to be the reason you can't concentrate."

What he doesn't know is he's too late. It's not the lack of sleep that gets me... it's thinking of him.

"Mia...I would love to see you again. Would you like to have dinner with me Friday evening?" he asks, then brings my hand up to his lips again.

"I would love to."

A broad smile widens across his face.

"Good. May I pick you up at 7:00 p.m."

"Yes. You may." I smile.

He kisses me, just like before. Again, I begin to feel like my legs are going to give out on me.

When he pulls away. He looks deep into my eyes.

"Until then Mia."

He lets my hand go and walks backwards a few steps, then turns around and walks away.

I'm left standing there, breathless and eager, wanting more. *Holy shit.*

As I see him turn the corner of the hall to go down the stairs, I gush with joy and smile.

I unlock my door and walk in. When I turn on my nightstand lamp, I see a written note from the dorm administrator.

Mia – A Tom Daniels called and said it's very important you call him. He said he called your cell a few times and left a message.

Shit! Sheriff Daniels! I forgot to take my cell phone off silent today.

I pull out my cell and see six missed calls all from the Sheriff and one voice message. I play the message and listen.

"Mia...it's uhm Sheriff Daniels. I need to talk to you about your parents. Uhm...I honestly don't know how to say this but...Ugh...I think it would be best if you just called me back. I've come across some new evidence, as well as...other information. It's very important you call me. Please...."

The message ends and I look at my phone not knowing what to think. I'm utterly confused.

"What the...? New evidence?!"

Sixteen

As soon as I make my way out of the dorm, I propel myself up and onto the rooftop. I see Lucius sitting by the backside keeping watch.

"Back already. I figured you and Mia would be chatting for much longer." Lucius says with a grin.

"A mongrel has been in her dorm. I smelt a lingering odor in the hallway, barely noticeable at first, but as we got closer to her door, I caught it."

Lucius stands, troubled by the news. "Impossible! We've both been keeping watch. Who was it brother?" Lucius asks with concern.

"I don't know. The smell was unfamiliar. No one we have ever encountered. Can you ask your contacts at the Council if they've made new orders, and if they've hired a new Scout to retrieve her?"

"The Council knows not to cross us. You really think they would send another after her?"

"No. Something seems off. I have a feeling whoever this is, isn't working under the Council's order, but we must be sure."

"If that's true brother, if others are after her now, we will need to inform the Keepers."

"Yes, I believe we must. Will you do me this favor Lucius, and make contact with them? I want to stay near her. I don't like that she is vulnerable like this."

"Are you sure it wasn't Brutus tempting his luck?"

"I'm sure. It was something quite different. Wild and untamed. Almost like that night."

"Do you want me to involve the Witch?"

"No. let us be sure of what we know before we alarm her. She will not be happy either way, but we shall stay clear of her so that she does not give us more orders."

"Dear the Gods. I like how you think. She's a feisty one. I can barely stand her."

"Easy Lucius. She loves Mia and only wants what's best for her."

"Yes, but she can do that without being a snob."

"I think you two are very similar. Maybe you two can't stand one another because you are so much alike."

"Pfft...I'm nothing like that Sorceress. The way she bosses us around as if we were her personal foot soldiers. I wish I could throw water on her and watch her melt."

I shake my head at how amusing it is to see Lucius so irritated.

"Will you be able to handle keeping watch from afar?" Lucius asks.

"Yes...yes. Go on. I'll be fine."

"Alright. I will go straight away to the Keepers. Try and remain calm brother. We will figure this out. I'll return a couple of days with news."

I watch Lucius leap down from the rooftop and vanish into the night.

I sit there for a while, thinking about all the ways I could fail her. Every time I touch her, I feel a connection to her I never thought possible. It's as if her soul sings in harmony to mine. And when I kissed her, it was the most powerful sensation I've ever encountered.

I wanted and needed every part of her. And to think I could fail her now, it's agonizing.

I've failed her once before and it kills me every day. I see her tormented by her parents' murder and I could have done something about it. Some days are better than others for her but she will never be what she once was.

I remember that day clearly as if it were yesterday. I was keeping guard while she was at her friend Mandy's house. I stayed within the shadows, watching her through the window, laughing carelessly and happily. There was light within her shining bright.

When she was leaving the house, she sensed my presence for the very first time. I've kept an eye on her since the day she was born, always close by. Never has she ever felt me, until that night.

When she peered into the night, looking for what might be lurking in the shadows, I realized then I felt something for her. It was if at that very moment, we connected.

Knowing she was on her way home, I went there first to scout the grounds, and that's when I smelled the mongrel. When I arrived, he had already taken the life of Leah and Sam. I had just caught him cleaning the knife with a towel, trying to hide his prints.

I thrusted myself forward and began pounding away at his face. He by chance got a grip of me and threw me. With that half second, he got up and ran towards the back exit. I lunged at him and held him imprisoned to the wall.

"Who sent you?" I said through gritted teeth.

He tried twisting and turning to break himself free, but I was stronger. I threw him down the hall and pounded his head against a Grandfather clock. I then picked him up over my shoulders and as I tossed him forward and pounced on his chest as he hit the floor.

"I'm not going to ask you again. Who sent you?!!" I growled out.

All he did was laugh. It was then that we both heard a car pull up. The mongrel looked pleased. He was here for her. Mia.

The thought put me into a dark rage. I grabbed him by the throat and dragged him out the back door and far into the back yard, hidden behind the trees.

"This is your last chance. Who sent you?"

"More will come for her. You won't be able to stop them all. You may kill me, but another will come for sweet little Mia. Had you not been here, I would have tasted her blood and ravaged her body." He laughed, while coughing up blood.

I saw nothing but a black soul with a dark thirst to kill. The thought of him touching Mia drove me mad. His laughter made me want to snap his neck, and so I did.

I dropped his dead body to the ground, looking at it with disgust.

I hear a cry from inside the house and I realized what Mia had return to.

I ran to the side of the house to peer through the kitchen window. That's where I saw it happen. I saw Mia's heart break into a thousand pieces. She was crying hysterically, pleading for her parents to awaken.

I hadn't felt pain for another in so long I had almost forgot what the feeling was like. My heart and soul grieved for her. I wanted to run inside and comfort her, but I couldn't. I was to remain in the shadows where I belonged.

I should have been there to save them, for her. Leah and Sam were good people and deserved better. They loved Mia, for she was their world. I watched them raise a beautiful young girl into a gorgeous woman, inside and out.

No one should have to suffer this way, especially not Mia. She has already had so much taken from her. Not again. And I was unable to stop it. I may have saved her life, but what life will she live enduring such pain and heart ache.

As much pain as she went through, the Vis remained dormant. I guess the spell that was enchanted on her worked well. But you can only hold nature back for so long before it takes it rightful place.

Mia is the only Saga that gained power from the Vis before she was sixteen years of age. Mia was only five when her power came to her, calling to be released.

Every year, the Keepers would enchant her to keep the Vis dormant until she was ready to wield it. When she was of rightful age, Mia's parents begged the Keepers to leave the Vis dormant. They wanted a normal and happy life for her. Mia was perfect in their eyes.

The Keepers agreed to the terms as long as her emotions were kept under control. Emotions drive power into the Vis, especially dark thoughts and emotions such as anger and despair.

After the death of Mia's parents, the Keepers kept a close eye on her to ensure the Vis did not break through. The Keepers used every ounce of power they had to restrain the Vis from seeping through Mia.

It was dangerous to allow its power to be released while she mourned. The heartache she felt would only feed the dark energy of the Vis. When dark energy is constantly released, it begins to consume the host, swaying the host to use it for evil instead of good. I can never imagine Mia becoming something dark. I won't allow it.

I look up at the night sky and ask the Gods to give me strength and courage to protect her. I pray I never let her down again. I pray I can be her saving grace.

Seventeen

As usual, I couldn't sleep last night. The Sheriff's message was lingering in the back of my mind telling me something isn't right. I decide it would be best to call the Sheriff after my classes. I don't want to worry about whatever the Sheriff has to say before my long day.

Thinking about my parents and what the Sheriff may have in store for me, reminded me that I need to call Cambridge and get in touch with the HR department. I've been meaning to get copies of everything they have on my parents to give to the Sheriff.

Sherriff Daniels has asked a couple of times. Once before I left for College, and in recent voicemails. I know it would be easier if I got them for him instead of him having to figure out how to Subpoena Cambridge. I put a reminder on my phone to do that and have snoozed it for three years now.

Getting my mind back on track and off the Sheriff's message isn't hard, it's getting my mind off Alex and our upcoming date that is worrying me. I haven't been on a date since my Senior year.

My last date was with David Hernandez, a good friend I'd known since elementary school. I had a crush on him for years and when Mandy finally got us together, it wasn't exactly what I hoped.

I think my expectations were way too high from all the angst of wanting to get with David, that when it finally happened, it was a huge disappointment. I was disappointed that he turned out to be just like every other guy out there, all about sex. I was hoping David would be different. I thought that since we'd known each other for so long and shared some secret crush for one another, we would have this great connection. There was absolutely nothing. It was a sad day for me.

After David, I just decided not to waste my time. Mandy tried so many times to hook me up with guys, but I always came up with excuses why I couldn't.

Mandy finally gave up on me and let me have things my way, of course until Prom. She forced it then. I gave in for that night only but didn't consider it a date. My so-called dance partner was a friend of Mandy's boy-toy Jason, who didn't even go to our school. Prom was just a party for him to crash. The only time he actually spoke to me was after Prom when he told me he had a hotel room. I think he ended up sleeping with another girl from Prom when I told him to go screw himself.

Mom always said I'm much more mature than most girls my age and that's why I don't give guys my age a chance. How could I disagree? It's absolutely true.

I think that's why I'm so drawn to Alex. He's different in so many ways. He's mature, mysterious, hot, sexy, and obviously smart. He's made a great life for himself at a young age and it takes dedication and hard work to do something like that. Although, for all I know he could still be your typical hit-it and quit-it kind of guy.

The more I think about Alex the more I begin to panic. What if I'm not anything like what he expects? What if he's everything I want in a guy and he wants nothing to do with me after tomorrow night? Do I really want to take the chance of getting my heart broken right now?

I don't know if I'll be able to handle something like that. Somehow, I've managed to keep my sanity, but I don't know how much longer I can keep this act up. I know everyone hits a breaking point. A second broken heart will certainly do that.

The day after my parent's murder, I remember waking up in the hospital, hoping everything that happened was a dream. I don't remember anything after finding my parents lying on the kitchen floor. From what the Sheriff said I was in absolute shock and no one could get through to me, that I was frozen and speechless.

The Sheriff said Mandy tried to communicate with me but couldn't get through to me either. I don't remember any of it. When I woke up in the hospital bed and saw Mandy and her mom on one side and the Sheriff on the other, I knew then, my dream was reality. I cried but nothing more. It seemed like I was in the twilight zone. I thought I would go home, and everything would go back to the way it was. My heart broken for the first time in my life from the depth of my loss. I realized I was alone and on my own.

I was thankful my parents taught me how to take care of myself early on. I learned how to cook and clean before I was even eight, and how to drive and manage money when I was thirteen. I basically took care of myself every day. They were there when I needed them, but left many decisions in my own hands, giving me the opportunity to make right or wrong decisions for myself.

I respected them so much for the freedom that I tried to make careful decisions. No other parent would give a child that much freedom and responsibility. I loved them for believing I would do the right thing.

As much as I wanted to curl up in a ball and sob for days after their death, I knew my parents wouldn't want that. They would want me to move on, grow up, and live my life like I was prepared to do.

So here I am. Three years sober from my pain. I can't break now. I can't let someone like Alex distract me from how well I've done. My heart is still fragile and I don't want it broken.

After really thinking about the date, I come to the decision that I should break it off. I don't need the diversion right now. I need to focus on my priorities and sadly Alex is not one of them.

I pull out my phone and decide I should just call him and tell him it's not going to work. Then I remember that he never gave me his number. *Crap!* I can't just cancel on him when he shows up to pick me up.

Unless I act like I'm dreadfully sick. *No way!* I wouldn't want Alex to see me look like crap for one. Two... I'm a horrible liar. He would be able to see it instantly.

I will just endure the evening and let Alex know that whatever we have going can't go any further than Friday night. I'm sure he'll understand. He doesn't seem like the monogamous type anyways. After Friday night, we'll go our separate ways.

***

Back in the dorm, I sit down at my desk and pull out my "To Do" list. At the top of my list is to call Cambridge. I need to request copies of my parent's employment records. Might as well get it done now before calling the Sheriff.

I set my MacBook on my desk and open my Google tab. I search University of Cambridge and look up their Human Resources Division. I find a number and dial the foreign number as listed and listen.

"University of Cambridge. How may I assist you?"

"Hi...my name is Mia Williams and my parents, who passed away three years ago, were employees of Cambridge. I would like to request a copy of their employment records. Could you tell me what your records request process is?"

"Let me forward you to the correct contact. Hold please."

I love hearing that English accent.

"Cambridge. This is Joanne"

"Hello Joanne. I'm looking to request a copy of my late parent's employment records. Could you please tell me what your records request process is?"

"Of course. First, let's verify employment. Can you tell me your parents' legal names?"

"Yes ma'am. Leah and Samuel Williams."

There was complete silence.

"Ma'am. You still there?" I ask.

"Oh...uhm..."

The line goes silent again. Joanne says nothing and I don't know what to make of it. *Does she know my parents personally?*

"Joanne?"

"Uhm...I better direct you to Dr. Osborne."

Dr. Osborne? How do I know that name? It takes only a moment and then I remember. *My mom's letter I posted the night of her murder.* Before I can contest, she transfers me to a ringing line.

"Mia?"

"Uhm...yes. Is this Dr. Osborne? Wait...how did you know my name?"

The line is silent again. I almost think we're disconnected until Dr. Osborne clears his throat.

"It's really not safe to talk on this line. Please trust me. DO NOT CALL HERE AGAIN! I will be in touch. I promise!"

The line goes dead, and I'm stunned by the outburst. What does he mean? Why isn't it safe? I don't understand. What the hell just happened? I want to call back and ask him what the hell he's talking about, but something tells me I should hold off.

How? Does he even know how to get in touch with me?

I stare at the computer wondering whether I should call Joanne back and get information out of her. She seemed to know something, but she also seemed just as reluctant as Dr. Osborne. I need to think this through.

I decide to call the Sheriff and find out what he knows.

"Sheriff Daniels speaking"

"Hello Sheriff. It's Mia. I got your message and I'm a little confused."

"I understand. I really didn't want to leave you a message but there have been a few "incidents" here since you left. I would rather we discuss it all in person. I was thinking of coming out to see you this weekend if you don't mind."

The tone in his voice when he said "incidents" has me worried. The Sheriff seems nervous or maybe anxious. I definitely need to see the Sheriff.

"You want to come to North Carolina?! I'm a little concerned. Can you elaborate a little more about what incidents have occurred?"

I can hear the tone of uncertainty in the Sheriffs silence.

"I really think it would be best to discuss the matter in its entirety in person Mia. I'm so sorry to make you wait until this weekend but for now, please don't worry about it. You'll soon hear everything."

"Okay..."

"I can book a flight and be there Saturday afternoon. Do you want to meet somewhere on campus?"

"Sure. Let's say 2:00 p.m. at the Quad?"

"That would be perfect....and Mia...we'll get this all figured out. I promise."

"Okay Sheriff. I gues I'll see you then."

After I hang up, I think about what "incidents" could have occurred that the Sheriff didn't want to talk about over the phone. I wanted to tell him about my conversation with Dr. Osborne but my shock sort of got the best of me. What could be going on that he would fly all the way out to see me?"

I get up from my desk and lay on my bed. My mind is on overdrive. First the phone call with Dr. Osborne and then the so called incidents. I just want to take a quick nap and sleep this drama off.

Eighteen

We are totally slammed. Mocha's has been extremely busy today. I came in for my shift and poor Mr. and Mrs. T were getting yelled at for the back up on orders. When they saw me walk in, the look of relief was written all over their face. *Note to self: prepare for the worst on Thursdays.*

I can't believe how many customers we've had. What the hell is going on today that everyone needs caffeine? Since Mocha's is so close to the campus, most of the customers are students.

As I walk around the tables to pick up empty cups and plates, I can see by the books that most of the students are pre-med. I know pre-med requires a bit more attention, I just didn't realize it can be this bad. I'm so glad I didn't choose pre-med. I would be cramming on a caffeine high like these kids.

I continue to gather empty dishes and hear the bell on the door ring, letting us know another customer has entered. *Oh no...not another one.* I turn to the door and see a young girl standing there with books in her hands, smiling at me. She looks so familiar and I stunned by her beauty. Long, thick, shiny black hair, beautiful dark olive complexion, and large bold gray eyes. Her beauty has half the men in the shop speechless as they stare.

I hear Mr. and Mrs. T say something in Romani to the girl and she replies. She waves at them and I realize it's their daughter Mr. T spoke of.

The girl then looks back at me, smiling, and walks up.

"Hello Mia. I'm Natalia Taragos. My parents have told me so much about you."

"It's nice to meet you." I look down at my full hands, and give her an apologetic look wishing I could hold out my hand for a proper greeting.

"Here. Let me help you. You really have your hands full there."

"Oh, you don't have to do that."

Natalia smiles at me and grabs the stack of plates from one of my hands and sets them on top of her books.

"Thank you." I say apprehensive but thankful for the help.

Natalia follows me behind the counter. We both set the dishes in the sink.

"Really...thank you for your help."

"No problem! It's the least I can do. My parents rave about how much they appreciate the help. They didn't anticipate this place to be as busy as it is. You came along to help them at the perfect time."

Looking down at her books I remember Mr. T telling me that she was too busy with school to help out at with Mocha's.

"So...are you a student at Duke?"

"Yes. I hear you are too. What's your major?"

"Honestly I haven't really put too much thought into yet. I know I love to read and write so maybe something having to do with both. My parents told me not to worry too much about the future because it could change. When we talked about College, they wanted me to keep an open mind to any and all possibilities and for me to just get my basics out of the way first."

A melancholy look appears on Natalia's face and she gives a quick glance at Mr. and Mrs. T, who are behind us, listening to our conversation.

I turn around to look at them and I see an apprehensive look on their face. They look at me, smile, and turn to face new customers. I can't help but feel like they know something I don't.

"Your parents sound wonderful. To be allowed the opportunity to make decisions for yourself at our age, at least my family, is hard to do." She says with a short smile.

I stand there silent, washing dishes not knowing what to say. It saddens me to think about my parents and that exact discussion.

We were eating dinner and I had a stack of acceptance letters sitting next to my plate. I was going through each one and weighing the pros and cons with my parents. We were all so happy that I had so many options to choose from.

That night I saw a light in my parent's eyes I've never seen before. They were so proud of me. I remember seeing my father grab my mother's hand and squeeze it, giving her a smile, acknowledging a job well done. I loved seeing moments like that between them.

"Are you working this weekend Mia?" she asks.

"Uhm...yes. Oh wait... well actually, that is something I need to talk to your parents about. I'm scheduled to work Saturday from morning until four, but I have some personal matters I have to take care of around 2 p.m. I was hoping to see if I could get off a little early."

Natalia gives me an interested look and then turns to her parents.

"I'm sure they won't mind. I could fill in for you. I'm actually ahead on my assignments." She says smiling.

I turn and look at her medical books.

"Pre-med?"

"Yes."

"Any specific specialized practice?"

"Hematology and Clinical Research." She answers nervously.

"Study of blood? Interesting. What made you choose that?" I ask optimistic.

"I hope to assist with finding cures to blood pathogens."

"Like Aids?"

"That is one among many, yes." she says looking down at her hands.

"That's great. I wish the best of luck. Not many people have a goal like yours. I think that's amazing." I say smiling at her appreciatively.

As I wash dishes, Natalia helps by rinsing. We talk about the amazing University, our classes and hectic schedules. Then we talk about things to do off campus, music, books, and other interests. We actually have a lot in common. We are both huge fans of Harry Potter. *Nerd alert!* We both love the variety of music from indie rock to Bach, and we both play the piano. We talk with such ease it's like we've known each other for years.

After Natalia and I finished the dishes, I turn to Mr. and Mrs. T and ask to them about taking off early Saturday. Natalia heard my conversation and offered her services for the weekend. Mr. and Mrs. T looked a little worried at first, but then gladly consented after I told them that I would be available for the late Monday shift I was scheduled off for.

***

The night quickly came to a close. Natalia and Mr. and Mrs. T were all in the back office talking while I began to clean up here and there. While cleaning off the counter, my urge to pee was killing me. I've been holding it way too long and need immediate relief. I don't want to leave the counter with no one watching so I decide to go to the back office to ask if Natalia can watch the front while I make a quick trip to the ladies room.

I walk up, about to knock on the door, but I hear Natalia arguing with Mr. and Mrs. T through the cracked door opening. I stand there contemplating if it's a bad time to ask and then I get caught up in the conversation.

"*Natalia...it is your duty. You "must" do this. You have no choice. This is who you are.*"

"*Momma...I can't. I won't. You are asking me to forever change a person's life. What if she doesn't want this? I will have to live with that guilt, not you or papa. I refuse. I don't care what the consequences are. Who are we to decide where the burden lies.*"

"Natalia! You do not have a choice! She will be in danger if you do not release her power." Mrs. T says.

"She will be in danger if I do. They've been hunting her since she was born. Releasing her power will only allow the others to find her. She should be allowed to choose whether she want this life. Momma...it's not fair that I, her long time friend, should be the one to take that choice away from her. Please don't ask this of me."

What in God's name are they talking about? Whose life are they forever going to change? I wish I would have heard the beginning of this conversation. I feel bad for eves dropping, but I wouldn't be listening if they would have just shut the door all the way. *Not my fault.*

Just as the conversation begins to get good, I'm distracted by a voice from up front.

Nineteen

"Hello?"

Crap! I didn't even hear the doorbell jingle. Dang it! I want to hear what this is about.

I walk up front and I'm shocked with a pleasant surprise. It's Noah.

"Hi..." he says.

"Hey..." I say.

God he is hot! His lean, solid, muscular stature just stifles his Aeropostale shirt. And I love the warn-out ball-cap turned backwards, a combination of rough, tough, and boyish.

"What are you doing here?" I say smiling.

Noah steps up to the counter, stretching his arms, deep into his pockets. Looking around and then at me.

"So...I was in the neighborhood shopping and I thought to myself. *I sure would like a hot cup of coffee.* Then I remembered that there's this place called *Mocha's,* that this great girl told me about, and on the plus side, I remembered that the great girl happened to be you and that you worked here. So...here I am."

"You were in the neighborhood shopping? This late? It's almost 11:00 p.m. I didn't know the shopping centers were open this late." I say playfully.

Smiling and biting his lip, he leans over the counter and gazes into my eyes.

"I guess that explains why all the doors were locked."

I can't help but giggle. Noah smirks and looks down, pleased with himself.

"I was actually down the road at one of the frat houses. When I drove by, I saw the open sign on. I thought it would be a perfect time to check this place out. And...I was hoping to see you again." He sounds so sincere.

I smile at him and he cocks his head to the side and smiles back at me.

Wow. He wanted to see me again. What luck have I come across?

"Frat house huh? Well you must have been up to no good at this hour."

"Me? Trouble? No way. I'm too far from home to get in trouble. The only trouble I can get into here is mixing plaids with stripes."

"Oh, so you were a trouble maker back home then?"

"Just a little. You know us Southern folks. We like to tip cows, race lawnmowers and steel tractors. It's a red-neck thug life."

He has me laughing hard now.

"I'm sure your thug life must have been hard to leave behind."

"Nah...I'm free of all the hooligans pressuring me."

"You are too much. I bet your family misses you and your sense of humor."

"My mom reminds me every day when she calls. It's getting to the point where I want to change my number."

I think about that, and how much I wish my mom was calling me every day driving me insane.

"It's hard to miss home right now." He says as he stares at me.

I feel flushed all over. I stand there silent and stunned like an idiot. I can't come up with anything. All I can do is stare back, into his beautiful hazel eyes, glistening gold with shimmers of emerald.

Here I am, tense from the energy between us, when Noah looks calm and collective.

I finally lose my hold when Natalia walks up. She looks at me and then Noah, watching us as we fidget.

Realizing she may have interrupted something, she quickly gets to the point of her appearance.

"Hey...I was just about to come tell you that you can go ahead and go for the night. My parents are going to update the books and I told them I would relieve you and finish cleaning. I figured it would be a good time for me to get to know how to work things around here since I may be working shifts here and there." She says smiling.

I give her an appreciative smile and then look at Noah.

"I can skip the late-night caffeine and drive you to your dorm." Noah says smirking.

I shake my head at Noah thinking of how cute he is and then turn to Natalia.

"Thanks Natalia. I appreciate it. I would argue staying but I'm exhausted. I guess I'll see you around."

"Of course." Natalia smiles and winks at me.

I untie my apron, pull it over my head, and hang it up on the wall hook.

I turn to Noah and hold up my finger.

"Uhm...it will just be a minute. I just have to run and get my bag."

I quickly run to the back and go into the ladies room, remembering how much I had to pee. When I come out, I go into the office and tell Mr. and Mrs. T. goodnight and remind them again that I'll be leaving early Saturday, but will be stay late Monday. When I come back up front, Natalia is picking up and Noah is leaning on the counter waiting for me.

"Okay...I'm ready."

We walk outside the front door and I watch him point his keys to a black restored, 1985, Chevy pick-up parked against the curb. Noah pushes a button on his key chain and the engine roars to life. *Push start? Nice.*

I'm stunned and awed by this magnificent beast. I first notice its obscene height. It has a lift kit and gigantic off-road tires. It's definitely a hot boy-toy. I look back at Noah with a huge smile on my face. I love how tough this makes him. But then my smile fades and I hesitate, wondering how I'm going to climb up into the cab without looking stupid or falling. He eyes me, then the truck, and slightly laughs.

"No worries, I'll help you up." He says smirking.

"Okay. Don't let me fall. It's likely to happen. Not all girls are graceful you know."

Noah closes in on me, standing over me, gazing down into my eyes.

"Don't worry. I won't let you go. You're safe with me." He whispers gently.

My breathing hitches.

I step back a little to draw a line between us. It's an instant reaction from this so unfamiliar territory. My nerves have been all over the place. Plus...I don't know much about Noah and I've already decided that I don't need distractions in my life right now.

Noah seems like a great guy, but I need to make sure that our relationship stays platonic. I don't want to give him the wrong idea. Even though nothings official between Alex and I, I don't want to get mixed up with two guys at the same time. As excited as I was to see him, I need to stay focused. No more flirting. Just friends!

Noah reaches up, opens the door, and then holds out his hand.

"I promise. I won't let you fall."

I take his hand and climb up and in.

The drive was pretty short since Mocha's is so close to the campus. After Noah helps me out, we sit on one of the benches outside the dorm and talk.

We talk about his family and home. We compare College to High School. We talk about things we like to do, food we love, hobbies, and music we can't live without. We could both talk about music all day long. Most of all we talk about books. It's nice to be able to talk to someone who loves literature as much as I do. Of course, Noah likes mystery and sci-fi books more than anything and I love old world charisma and romance.

Before we know it, it's 2 a.m. I didn't realize it until the overwhelming feeling of wanting to fall asleep hits me and I yawn.

"Whoa. I didn't even realize it was this late." Noah looks at his watch and shakes his head disapprovingly.

"I'm so sorry. I didn't mean to keep you up. I can only imagine how tired you must be. I better get to my frat house too."

Noah looks just as tired.

"I didn't even think about it. We were so deep in thought about the mysteries of...wait...what were we talking about?" I tease.

"Oh I see. I'm boring you. I understand if you can't hang. Sci-fi mystery books aren't for everyone. You have to be super smart to read those kinds of books."

"Then why do you read them?"

"Touché!" Noah smirks at me and grabs my side to tickle me.

I giggle and almost snort from being so tired. He stops and looks at me trying to hide his smile.

"Don't laugh...or judge. I'm super sleepy."

He shakes his head and intently gazes into my eyes.

"Well...you better get to bed then. I would hate for you to pass out on me. That would be the first time I bored someone to sleep. Not good for the record books. And then I would have to leave you here and cover you up with newspaper."

I giggle again but I'm so tired that I can barely keep my eyes open.

"Ha...ha...Okay. I'm taking your advice. I'm going to drag myself to my bed."

Twenty

Noah gently helps me up and holds me still.

I look up into his eyes, once again mesmerized by their glow and hold my breath.

"I guess I'll see you around?" Noah looks at me as if he's waiting on me to do something.

It takes me a minute to form words as I'm lost in the warmth of his eyes.

"Ye-kay." I pause for a second and look around confused to what just came out of my mouth.

What was that?

"Sorry. I think I was trying to say yes and okay together. Yes. I will see you around."

Noah smiles at me and pushes a strand of hair behind my ear.

"You're too cute..." he says with a big smile.

I bite my lip and look down trying to hide my smile from his comment.

"Okay. I'll see you in class." Noah pulls his remote start from his pocket and fires up what I now call THE BEAST. He begins to walk off and then stops to turn toward me.

"Mia....do you have a boyfriend?"

Oh no. What do I say? Say yes! NO...horrible liar. Crap!

"Uhm...no."

"You didn't sound too sure." He says laughing.

"I don't...but I am going on a date tomorrow night."

The look on Noah's face is pure disappointment. He drives his hands deep into his pockets and gives me a sincere smile.

"Well...I'll see you tomorrow Mia. Good night."

"Good night."

Noah jumps up and into his truck and drives off pretty quickly. The feeling of disappointment is overwhelming. All I said was I have a date. I'm not marrying the guy. But I understand. This is a good thing. Friends. Ugh...

I walk up the stairs dragging my feet, so tired. At the top I pull out my keys and begin walking to my door. I look down the hallway behind me and the lights are flickering at the end. I turn back around and ignore the scary look of it and get to my door. I put my key in the knob and I stop, feeling as if someone is watching me. As I turn to my right towards the flickering light, for once I'm not crazy.

There's someone standing at the end of the hallway...watching me. I can't make out who it is. All I can see is their dark shape and that it's a man. I nervously try and unlock the door, but my hands feel weak and sweaty. I look back towards the figure and I start to freak out as I see him walking my way.

"Shit!"

Come on Mia! Calm down. Just relax and open the door.

I twist and turn and stupidly I keep locking the door instead of unlocking. Finally, the door opens, and I rush through and close it behind me. I lock the deadbolt and the chain just in case. I stand back looking at the light beneath the door waiting to see a shadow, but nothing appears.

I finally get the courage to look through the peep hole and thankfully I see nothing. I keep looking and nothing still.

I step back to think a moment.

Maybe he went down the stairs.

I look one last time and again nothing.

I step back and walk to my bed. I throw my bag to the floor and sit down.

I am really losing it. I have got to get a grip of myself. Geeze...relax Mia.

I wait a few minutes, staring at the door, letting my nerves ease and finally I lie down. I look over towards Bianca and notice she's not in bed. She must be with Rent-a-Cop.

As I lie in bed my body begins to sink in to place and relax. Within in minutes I'm sound asleep.

I wake to the door slamming open against the chain. I jump up terrified that someone is trying to get in. I curl up in the corner of my bed and look around for something to use to as protection. I see scissors on the desk and get ready to run for them when I hear Bianca.

"Mia...open the door! Why the hell do you have the chain on the door?"

Shit! Bianca.

"I'm so sorry Bianca. Hold on one sec."

I walk up to the door and close it to take the chain off.

As I open the door Bianca looks half a sleep and half drunk.

"Mia...rule of thumb." She says as she waves her thumb across her face fascinated by it.

I giggle and bite my lower lip to shut myself up.

"You don't use the chain lock when your roommate is out. You never know when they'll be sneaking back in." She says slurred.

I smile at her nodding my head at the now new roommate rule.

"I'm sorry. I saw you weren't here, but I was so tired that I forgot to undo the chain."

Bianca stumbles past me and throws herself on her bed.

"What time is it?" I ask her as I wonder where she was.

"Time for sleep. I night...night."

I barely understand Bianca's funny statement with her face in her pillow.

I look at the clock and its 3:20 a.m.

Ugh...

"Bianca...You're going to suffocate yourself lying like that."

I get no response except for Bianca's snoring.

I laugh at how crazy she can be. I can only imagine what she was doing. How she is ever going to make it through one more year of school and partying I have no idea.

I grab Bianca and try and turn her to her side. She willingly turns all the way over and snores louder.

I laugh and think of getting my phone to take a video. I could use it as leverage. But I'm way too tired and I just want to crawl in bed and go "night...night" myself.

Before getting in bed, I take off my clothes and change in a tank and shorts since I fell asleep in my work clothes.

I pull my duvet back and crawl into bed. The warm feeling of the duvet and the fluffiness of my pillow is exactly what I needed. Bianca's snoring doesn't even bother me at this point.

My tired body gives out and again, I fall fast asleep.

Twenty-One

I pace back and forth on the rooftop, fuming. First a boy flirting with Mia and now a mongrel. The fury inside me wants to rip the mongrel apart, piece by piece.

Watching Mia and that boy Noah, flirting with one another drove me insane. I wanted to jump down and wrap my hands around the boy's throat and squeeze the life out of him.

Who does he think he is? This halfwit country boy.

I snarl comes out of my mouth and realize I'm losing control. I can't allow my emotions to interfere. I must remain calm so that I can question the mongrel.

Besides, Mia is allowed to befriend anyone she chooses. I have no right to be angry. I've done this to myself by getting involved. She's a college student. What do I expect? For her to ignore every advance a young male makes, and close herself off from the world?

I know the right answer, but I can't help thinking about how much I'd prefer she did close herself off from the world so that I can have her to myself. But I know that's selfish. I'm being irrational. I'm acting...jealous.

By the Gods.

What has become of me? I'm acting like a mad man. I've never encountered this feeling before. I've seen what jealousy can do to people and I never understood it.

I could never grasp how an emotion like jealousy could drive a person to behave so foolish and unpredictable. Now I do.

I hear the mongrel trying to speak through the sack over his head.

"Shut it or I'll cut your tongue out!" I kick him while he lays on the ground with his hands tied behind his back.

When I first watched her step out the front door of Mocha's with Noah, laughing and smiling, I wanted so badly to appear and give some pathetic excuse for why I needed to see her so she wouldn't go with him. But all I did was watch from afar and clench my jaw so tight I tasted blood.

And when they locked eyes for a moment, I felt this pain in my gut, like I was wounded. I guess in a way I was wounded. I saw how she looked at him and it hurt me deeply. I want to be the only one she looks at that way. Like she sees something she desires.

When he helped her get into that ridiculous monstrosity of a truck, I pulled my sword, ready to pounce and slice away at his fingers.

All I could think about is how he had his filthy hands on her. I wanted to take her away and hold her close to me. It should be my hands on her, gently holding her by her tiny waist. Not him.

I watched and listened for hours as they talked about what they like in music, food, hobbies and books. I was envious of him. He was able to get to know her so simplistically. I knew all of these things about her, but from lurking in the shadows.

He has the ability to befriend her and spend quality time with her. I will always be hidden from her, unable to be there for her the way he can.

When Noah asked if she had a boyfriend, it peeked my interest to hear what she would say. When she announced she didn't, I unreasonably got upset. Of course, I'm not her boyfriend so I mustn't hold that against Mia. I'm just glad she made it clear she has a date tomorrow, with me no less. The purest form of pleasure swept across me when I saw country boy pout and walk away afterwards.

But then I was annoyed and angry that country boy lost his manners by not walking Mia up to her room, leaving her in the dark alone late at night. Luckily for him, I'm here keeping an eye on her.

I watched as poor sleepy Mia walked into her dorm. When I jumped down from the rooftop, I decided to go up and make sure she made it in. That's when I smelt the dirty mongrel again.

I ran up the stairs and just as he was heading in her direction, I grabbed him and pulled him down the stairs, choking him unconscious. He was lucky I didn't snap his neck in two, but I need answers.

I pull the bag off his head and sit him up. I give him a look over and I don't recall ever seeing him before.

"Who are you?" I ask.

"I don't have to tell you nothing."

"Well...I think we can both agree you lack education by way of your double negatives. So, I think we can cross off student from the list. Who sent you after Mia?"

The mongrel remains quiet.

"I have no patience dog. I will peel the flesh from your bones if I must and I will have. Now, let's start over. Who sent you?"

"You can do whatever you want fang boy. You don't scare me. I've been through it all. We all knew the sacrifice we would have to pay. I gladly give my life for my pack. That girl has two choices. Grant us command over her Vis or die."

"Wrong answer." I grab ahold of his wrist tied behind his back and break it.

He howls from the pain and then begins to laugh.

"He's coming for her. One way or another, he will have her. She will belong to him because soon he will have what he needs to control her."

"Impossible. It was lost over a thousand years ago and no one knows where it is."

He laughs. "Her parents knew. What do you think they've been working on all this time? Who do you think they've been working for? They found it and tried to keep it hidden."

I pull back his head and glare into his eyes.

"You lie dog. They would never put Mia in danger."

He laughs and spits up blood. "They had no choice. They made a deal with the devil and the devil wanted payment. When they refused to pay up, they paid the price."

He begins laughing hysterically. "She'll be ours soon. We will have ultimate control over everyone. She is going to be our weapon now."

Before I can choke the life out of him, he grinds his teeth together and I see black foam forming in his mouth. His eyes roll back, and his body begins convulsing. In a matter of seconds, he's dead.

"Shit!"

I dig through the mongrel's clothes hoping to find something that will give me a clue but I find nothing. Not even a cell phone or wallet. He's a nomad vagrant, just like Brutus said. They keep nothing for themselves and live in the wild. They steal money and phones from strangers to check in with their pack leaders. No trace left behind.

What he said can't be true. The Visceral stone was lost during the war and has been lost ever since. Many have tried looking for it, hoping to obtain its power and power over the Saga. Whomever finds the stone can wield its power to control the Saga for their bidding.

I can't let this happen. I must let Lucius know so that he can find out more from the Keepers and the Council.

If this is true, we are all in danger. Mia most of all. I refuse to let her be a puppet. Whoever is after her, will face my fury.

Twenty-Two

TGIF!! I've been swamped with assignments all week and I'm ready for a weekend break.

Walking back to Campus from lunch with an achingly full stomach, I think about the "date" I have with Alex tonight. Where he's going to take me, what to wear, and why I ate so much when I should be watching my figure since I've been on a ramen noodle cup diet. Most of all, wondering if Alex is even going to show. What if I get all dressed up and I end up sitting around waiting on Alex all night for him not to show. I don't even know why I'm wasting my time with him. *We really should have exchanged numbers.*

Making my way to class I see Noah on the opposite end heading the same way and I light up. We catch up to each other and we give each other a big goofy smile. I playfully push him with my shoulder, and he does the same to me. We turn into class and begin trailing up the stairs to the seats we sat in last.

"How did you sleep?"

"Good. You?"

"I knocked out as soon as I hit the bed." Noah says smiling.

"Yeah...me too. This week has been sort of crazy. So many assignments. I feel like they just keep piling on. I love writing but by the end of this year I may change my mind." I say pouting.

"Same here. I'm ready for Spring Break."

"Less than two months." I wine.

"I know...Sucks!" Noah says yawning. Poor guy looks as tired as I do.

We make our way up to our seats in class and pull out our notepads and books. Noah digs around in his bag looking for a pen to write with and before he can give up, I pull an extra pen out and hand it to him.

"You know...you should really be more prepared." I say winking at him.

"Why when I sit next to someone like you. I'm sure you have your pens and highlighters color coordinated."

I bite my lip and scrunch up my nose at the thought. Then I pull out two small baggies to show him he's right.

"Dear Barbara..."

I laugh at the Dodgeball quote and shake my head.

"You actually color coordinated all your pens and highlighters. Wow. OCD much?" he says with a smoldering smile.

"No. I just like to be organized and prepared. There's a huge difference."

Noah puts his hands in the air with defeat.

"Hey...I'm a smart guy. I know the rule. Women always have to be right."

"Don't you mean "are" always right?"

"Whichever you prefer."

I shove Noah and he grabs his arm.

"Man...you're aggressive. Always so pushy. There's anger management for that."

I laugh at him and then put my finger to my lips, telling to him to quiet down as the professor steps up to the podium.

While the Professor lectures, Noah continues our banter by passing notes.

We first entertain ourselves with a page full of Tic-Tac-Toe. Once we realize we're both way too smart to out-smart one another, we give up and move on to hangman.

Noah starts off with his first word being "BORED". After I figure it out Noah takes the note from me and writes:

I am beyond BORED. Let's sneak out?

When Noah passes the note back to me, I laugh and quickly cover my mouth trying to keep myself quiet. I then create my own hangman game and pass it to Noah to figure out. After almost a dozen letters Noah finally figures out the word "TROUBLE". When Noah passes it back to me, I write:

You are TROUBLE! I should stay away from you.

I pass the note back to Noah and he reads it with a smirk on his face. He leans to his right and looks down at me.

"I don't think I could bare it if you did. Besides, when you have trouble sleeping, I'm the guy to call. All I have to do is give you a narrative of Space Commander."

I giggle and smile at Noah. We stare at one another and I can feel something between us, but it's nothing like the intensity I feel with Alex. There's an electric vibe between Noah and I, but I feel as if there's something Alex has that keeps my mind going back to him. Thinking about Alex makes me break our moment and I look away.

"Sadly Noah, I think that's a talent shared by many other Nerds."

Noah laughs but before Noah can respond, the Professor dismisses the class, and everyone begins to leave.

While I put my book in my bag Noah has this questionable look on his face.

"What's wrong?" I ask him.

"Are you still going on your date tonight?" He looks concerned.

"So far that I know. Why?"

Noah nervously puts his hands in his pockets. Which is the cutest thing.

"Just wondering. So...how do you know the guy? The one you're going on a date with?"

I think about how I'm going to answer that.

"I uh met him here on campus."

"Oh...he goes here too?"

"Uhm actually no. He was on campus for business. We just sort of ran into one another."

"Oh...is he older?" Noah asks.

"A little. Not by much. Look Noah...we barely know each other. I doubt I'll see him again after tonight. I don't think he's from around here. I only agreed because I thought it would nice to get out."

"Well...be careful with this guy you "barely" know Mia. There are some freaks out there and you just never know."

"I will. Besides I haven't been on a date in a long time. I might trip and fall flat on my face and make a fool of myself which will end the date fairly quickly."

Noah hides a smile and nods his head like it's possible.

"I can totally see you doing that."

"Hey..." I pout.

"I'm kidding. Look...just be yourself. If the guy doesn't instantly fall for you, he's the fool."

I smile at Noah's sweet compliment.

"Well...I better go. I'll see ya later."

Noah smiles and quickly heads down the stairs before I can say another word.

I grab my bag and drag myself down the stairs sulking.

Noah is funny, charming, drop dead gorgeous, and here I am making myself unavailable for someone I know nothing about. I know more about Noah than I do Alex. I feel so at ease with Noah. He's your boy next door kinda guy. But there's something about Alex that I'm drawn to. He's so different from anything I've ever known. When I'm around him I feel like there's some invisible energy between us that pulls us together. It scares me, but that only drives me to want to figure it out.

When I open the dorm room door Bianca is standing by her bed wrapped in a towel and blow drying her hair. She stops the dryer and says hello and then continues. I drop my bag to the floor and make my way to my bed and lie down. This day has been exhausting.

"Hey...do you want to go out with us tonight? Heather and I are going to that bar *Escape*. Wanna come with?" Bianca anxiously smiles.

"No thanks. Why do you go to Bars when there is always a party to go to somewhere around campus?"

"Because it's the same frat boy idiots at every party. I'm over it. Are you sure you don't want to come with?"

"I actually have a date tonight."

Bianca looks at me surprised.

"Really? With who?"

I sit up with an utterly pathetic look.

"Some guy I met. What am I going to do? He is totally out of my league. He's rich and hot. Pretty much seems to have it all, and for some odd reason he wants to take me out on a date." I throw myself back and cover my eyes with my arm.

"The worst part is there's another really hot guy in my Creative Writing class I like too and I think he likes me."

I feel Bianca sit at the end of the bed.

"Mia...if this is your biggest problem, I think you'll survive. I mean are you listening to yourself? Two really hot guys like you. What's the problem? I say date AND screw them both and decide after which one to keep."

"Bianca!" I sit up and throw my pillow at her. She laughs and throws her hands up.

"Or I can help you out. I can totally take one off your hands."

I grab my other pillow and toss it at her, and it dead pans her right in the face and we both laugh.

"Question. So, do you think he'll want to have sex on the first date?" I ask.

"Uhm...guys want to have sex with you as soon as they lay eyes on you. That's all they think about. You always end up sleeping with them on the first night. How many dates have you been on that don't end up that way?"

"Hm...like a dozen. The last time I went on an official date was my Senior year in High School. I didn't screw him on the first date either."

The look on Bianca's face is priceless.

"Seriously?"

"Guys in high school are pretty immature."

Bianca rolls her eyes at me.

"Sorry to break it to you sweetheart but that doesn't change after high school. They are all immature no matter how old."

"What if Alex wants to have sex tonight?"

Bianca looks at me like that was the stupidest question ever.

"You have sex. What's the problem?"

Before I can say anything, she jumps up off my bed and faces me.

"Holy shit! You're a fucking virgin!!"

Twenty-Three

Are you kidding me? Oh my God!!! I didn't think your kind still existed at our age!"

Bianca stands and looks at me bewildered.

"Gee...thanks. Why not scream it a little louder for the whole campus to hear." Not this again. I've had this chat with Mandy many times before. Mandy suddenly becomes a Nike commercial...*Just do it!*

"Why are you still a virgin? I think the last time I met a virgin was my freshman year of high school. Are you secretly religious?"

"You act as if I'm some sort of rare species. No, it's not because I'm saving myself for marriage or anything." My tone comes out a little harsh.

"I'm sorry this is just...I mean you have all the goods and you're...normal. Why haven't you given it up?"

"I don't know. Mainly fear. I was scared. I've come close a couple of times but then I would freak out and never talk to the guy again."

"Dude...you have no idea what you're missing out on. Wow...a virgin..."

"Bianca! This isn't helping me." I sit on my bed holding my knees wondering if I should just call the whole thing off.

"I think I'm just going to pretend that I'm sick and forget the whole thing."

Bianca sits back on my bed and runs her hand down my hair and smiles sincerely.

"Oh honey. If this is how you act before a date, then I can see why you're still a virgin. Look Mia...I think it's SUPER that you've held on to your virginity and all, but you're never going to get out and meet guys with this sort of fear. Just tell this "Alex" guy that you want to take things slow. Don't tell him you're a virgin though. You will become his new conquest if you do. If he doesn't understand, then forget him and move on. He's no gentlemen if he can't respect your wishes. If you decide that you want to have sex, then go for it. You're an adult now."

Bianca's right. I am an adult now and I should just get it over with. I was scared of having sex in high school for the fear of word getting out and showing up on the 5:00 o'clock news, or getting pregnant while I was in high school, or catching some really gross disease. Now that I'm out of high school, I don't have to worry about an entire school spreading the word about me losing my virginity or asking my parents if I can get on birth control, which I ended up doing my Senior year anyway, the point is...this is College. No one cares right?

"I guess it's sort of neat that you've held on to your virginity this long. My first was with a guy I really fell for my freshman year. We were together for like six months. Soon after we did it, he broke up with me. I was pretty heart broken. All I thought about was how I gave him every part of me. So now...I basically think like a dude. Not giving a shit about what the other person wants. I know it sounds fucked up, but it's me protecting myself." Bianca looks down and shrugs her shoulders trying to hide her feelings.

"What about when the right guy comes along and falls hard for you?" I ask sympathetic to her plight.

Bianca smiles thinking about the idea.

"I'll think about it when the time comes. For now, I'm just having fun."

I shake my head at the idea.

"Don't worry. I'm careful. I use protection all the time and I'm on birth control just in case." She says shrugging her shoulders.

I hug my knees and let it all sink in. Do I want to have sex with a guy who might drop me the next day? That would suck!

"Look...you'll be fine. You don't have to do anything you don't want to do."

I'm so thankful to have Bianca here with me. I dated here and there in high school but nothing too serious. The few times that I felt like things were getting hot and heavy with a guy I would back off, scared of where it could lead. My Junior and Senior year I just didn't have a lot of time for guys. I was always way too busy.

"Your right. It's just a date. Who has sex on the first date anyway?" I say incredulously.

Then realizing what I just said I turn to look at Bianca who is scowling at me.

"Sorry. I forgot."

We both laugh and shake our heads at the thought.

"So...what are you going to wear tonight?"

"Not sure yet. I have a few ideas in my head, but I don't know where we are going."

"I say wear a sexy dress. You can't go wrong with a dress."

I think about that and agree.

"Okay...dress it is. I did bring a few with me from home."

I get up and walk to my wardrobe and open it. I see four dresses. One black and white chevron maxi, one short black dress, one deep blue midi strapless, and one short summer floral. Then I look at my sweaters and cover ups to see which one I could wear with one of the dresses. I figure it out and decide I better hit the shower once more to shave my legs, under arms and bikini area.

When I return from the shower Bianca is already fully dressed and looking gorgeous as usual. Hair, makeup, nails, all to the max. She's wearing a red fitted strapless romper and black stilettos.

"You look amazing Bianca. Red really suits you."

"Thanks doll!" She winks and blows me a kiss.

"I have plenty of time to help you get ready. Do you want me to spiral your hair? I think it would look great down and with a few loose wavy curls."

"Sure! I'll work on my makeup in the meantime. Thanks B!"

Having Bianca here to help me makes me miss Mandy. She was always there to help me get ready for any big events. It feels weird without her. She and Bianca would get along great. I guess this is just how growing up works though.

After an hour of primping, I'm ready to go. My hair is spiraled, smoky eye makeup done, and nude lip gloss to finish it off. I decided to wear my fitted blue strapless midi, my black faux leather biker jacket, and black high heel booties.

"You look hot doll!" Bianca claps her hands.

"If Mr. Dreamy doesn't want to screw you tonight, he's got a problem because I even want to hump you." Bianca comes up to me and starts her Night at the Roxbury bump and I laugh and fall onto my bed.

"You're going to break your hip...or mine doing that."

"Tell me about it. I think I felt your hip bone." She says laughing.

"Okay I better get out of here. I'm sure Heather is getting pissed waiting on me. Good luck NOT getting laid tonight." Bianca winks at me and grabs her purse to leave. When she opens the door, Alex is standing there.

Bianca steps back and her smile drops to just an open mouth as she's mesmerized by my "Mr. Hottie".

"Pardon me. I was just about to knock. I'm here to see Mia."

Bianca slowly turns to look at me and then back to Alex.

"Oh...of course. Let me grab her. She'll be right with you." Bianca closes the door and runs up to me.

"Bianca...why did you close the door on him? I'm ready."

"Oh...my...God! Mia! You have to sleep with him! He's not dreamy, he's fucking steamy. Let Mr. Steamy pop that cherry and then tell me every detail."

My mouth is wide open from her outburst.

"Bianca! He can probably hear you. Be quiet!!"

"I hope he can so he knows what to do to you."

"Shhhhhh..." I grab her and cover her mouth.

Bianca pulls my hand down and smiles at me.

"Awww...my little virgin is going to come back a woman tonight."

"Shhhhh...you have got to stop. I'm leaving now."

"Well...have fun!" she says with a sexy shoulder roll.

I roll my eyes and grab my purse. I take a deep breath and open the door.

Alex is pacing the hall in front of the door and looks worried until he sees me.

"Wow. You...look amazing" he says almost horse, gulping.

"Thank you." I nervously look down at my clutch purse and then turn to close the door. When I turn back around, I remember why I agreed to the date.

Alex looks amazing. He's wearing a pair of off-the-hip black jeans with a fitted grey sweater and his black leather bomber jacket I love.

"You look great yourself." I gesture towards him.

"I'm sorry for the wait. My friend Bianca was just...making sure I had everything I needed."

Alex looks down and smiles as if he knows what we were talking about.

Shit. I hope he didn't hear Bianca.

Alex holds out his arm. "Shall we then?"

Twenty-Four

Alex leads me down the stairs and to the parking lot where we walk up to a navy-blue classic *James Bond* car.

"What kind of car is this?" I ask curiously looking through the window of the passenger side.

"365 Porsche. 1962 model." He says as he looks over the beautiful masterpiece sliding his hand over it as if he's rubbing a pet.

"It's gorgeous. I've never seen anything like it."

Alex smiles and opens the passenger door for me. "Not as gorgeous as you Mia." Alex takes my hand and kisses the top of it gently. I shudder and stare into his eyes, loving the glow of his sapphire jewels.

Then I begin to giggle as I think about how many times he's used that line on other girls.

"What's so funny?" Alex asks perplexed.

"Oh nothing. Just wondering how many times you've used that line on other girls." I say jokingly.

Alex's face diminishes to something more sincere. "I'm not the kind of guy you think I am Mia."

"Oh...and what kind of guy are you then?" I ask boldly.

"I don't particularly have time for women. I live a very complicated life, if that's what you would call it." He says as he moves my hair over my shoulder, resting his hands on my shoulders, rubbing his thumb across my collar bone.

I watch as his adamas apple bobs when he swallows. My body begins to melt at his touch and I close my eyes at the soft gentle caress. I try to bring myself back to reality by thinking about what he just said.

"Then how is it you have time for me Alex?"

Smirking he lifts my chin so that I'm looking up at him. "There's something special about you Mia. I would like to make time."

Alex brings his lips to mine, a smooth collide. He holds my face ever so gently and delves his tongue into my mouth and I willingly open. The delicious taste and warmth of his tongue is so alluring and pleasurable that chills run up my spine, and my legs feel like jelly. I wrap my arms around his neck bringing him closer wanting more of him. It all feels so overwhelming. I'm spell bound by his touch. I could kiss Alex like this forever.

When Alex pulls us apart, he has to steady me for I feel like I could fall over.

"Wow." I say

"Yes, wow." Alex agrees.

Alex takes my hand and gently kisses the top of it again.

"Let me help you in. The car sits a little low."

Boy he wasn't kidding. The car does sit low, and I almost wish I would have worn skinny jeans instead. Though after seeing Alex stare at my nicely sheen shaven legs from my dress being hiked up, I'm glad I picked the dress.

"So, what restaurant are we going to?"

"Actually...I have dinner waiting for us at my place. A good friend who is a Siu chef has agreed to prepare our meal for tonight."

"Wow. That sounds amazing. I just hope you're not some serial killer and I'm not the actual meal. Your real name isn't Hannibal Lector is it?"

Alex smiles at my joke and winks.

"That isn't exactly the answer I was looking for Alex."

Alex reaches for my hand and kisses it. A new favorite of mine.

"I could never think of harming you Mia. But I will say, the way you look in that dress, I could certainly devour you."

I stare into his eyes and I know my cheeks have given me away. I'm bushing by the thought of him devouring me.

We arrive on the outskirt of downtown Durham and pull into the garage of an old four-story building. The building looks as old as the town, but once we pull into the basement garage, I can see the building has been renovated.

Alex walks around the car and opens the door for me and we walk up to an open elevator. Alex puts in a key code on number pad and then pushes the button for the first floor. He then grabs a hold of my hand and kisses it as he did before. The elevator rises and just a few seconds later, the doors open and I'm blinded by the golden shimmer of light.

As soon as we exit the elevator, we are in his Foyer where an oval Persian rug is centered at the bottom of a beautifully handcrafted Mahogany staircase to our left. To our right, is a 10-foot cast iron door with metal rope lining the border. It looks as if it came straight from the Medieval times. When I look up, the golden light shimmering down on me is coming from a bronze and crystal Chandelier. It feels like old world charm.

As I view the open landscape of the first floor, I see what looks to be a study or sitting room, where a fire is lit. Leather and antique furniture, oil paintings and dark woods furnish the room. Golden lit sconces throughout the walls, give the rooms a Renaissance and romantic warm feeling. It's warm and inviting.

"This is so beautiful. Did the condo come like this?" I ask still spinning around, taking in every detail.

"No. I had some work done. It was an empty canvas. The only thing really original to the building is its brick walls."

Alex slowly walks around the room with his hands in his pockets, proud of the home he's made.

"Tell your interior designer I said...Wow!"

Alex smirks at me. "Why thank you."

"Wait, you designed and decorated this place?" I'm astonished. Most guys can't even pick out a clean shirt to wear.

"Every detail. Most of the paintings and furniture pieces I had at my home in Orvieto, just outside of Rome. I had it all shipped here so it could feel like a piece of home."

"Rome? You typically live in Italy?" I'm jaw dropped.

"Home is where I make it Mia. I travel quite a bit. However, if I were to call a place my home, it would likely be Orvieto."

"Is that where you're from?" I'm very curious now.

"It is." Alex' jaw tightens, and I can see he doesn't want to say much more.

"Honestly, I thought you were English. Your accent sounds English sometimes."

"I went to school in London and actually lived there for many years. You grow accustom to speaking proper English." He says with a smile.

"Oh, like boarding school or something? That's really amazing. I've never been outside of the US. I have my passport but no stamps."

"Come. Let's talk more over dinner."

Alex takes my hand and leads me past the staircase and down a hall, into the formal dining room. There we find a candlelit table for two and his Siu Chef friend putting the last touches on our meal.

This room is magnificent. The entire room is lined with an ash colored brick, including the ceiling. The doorways are rounded and held steady with thick wood beams. On one side of the wall are built in cubbies where hundreds of bottles of wine are held in place.

"Alex. How are you my friend?" the gentleman with an accent asks.

Alex reaches to shake the man's hand.

"Very well. Thank you. Mia...this is Edmond Bourcier. He is a legendary Siu Chef specializing in French cuisine."

I extend my hand to shake his.

"Very nice to meet you Edmond. Dinner looks amazing."

Edmond takes my hand and kisses the top. "Mon plaisir Mia."

"We have Bouillabaisse, Duck Confit, and Crème Brule for dessert."

"Well...I take my leave Alex...Mia. Bon appetite."

Edmond bows and then leaves the room. Alex leads me to my chair and pulls it out for me to sit. He walks around to the other side, never leaving his gaze from mine.

"Wow...this looks delicious. You really went all out. A Siu Chef in your home. That must have cost you a fortune." I say timidly.

"Not at all. Edmond owed me a favor and was happy to repay me." He says smirking.

"Shall we dig in?" Alex asks.

"Yes, please. I'm suddenly famished."

During dinner we talk about my new job and school. Alex seems very interested in what I have to say and it's definitely different from what I'm used to. After dinner Alex leads me to the living room where we sit near the fire place and have a couple of glasses of wine. I don't know much about wine but whatever I'm drinking is really delicious, and I can't seem to get enough.

We continue to talk about Duke and why I love writing, but after a while, I realize we've talked a lot about me and hardly about him.

"So...I feel like I've bored you to death about school and work. What about you? What's it like being you?" I say smiling, a little buzzed.

Alex looks down at his glass and then back to me where I see a sparkle from the fire ignite his eyes. I don't know if it's the wine or the room, but I feel very flushed and heated all over by the way he looks at me.

Alex grabs my glass and puts both our glasses down on the table next to him. He pulls me close to him and turns me around to where I am lying against him.

"I think we should slow down on the wine. A few more glasses and you may have to stay the night with me."

Just thinking about staying the night with Alex has me both excited and nervous. My heart begins to race and my thighs coil from the idea. I'm actually glad he took the wine away. I don't think I'm ready to be with him that way. Especially on our first date.

"Yeah...good idea. I do have to work in the morning." I say with a nervous giggle.

Alex gently rubs his hand up and down my arm and I sink into him loving his touch.

"So, tell me a little about where you are from." He asks.

"I thought it was time to talk about you?"

I've been fortunate enough to not have to talk about home so far and I'm not quite sure where to begin because it will only lead to the one thing I've been trying to hide from.

"I love hearing about you." He says while caressing me.

I'm not ready to go there. I don't talk about home at all because it eventually leads to the worst part of my life.

"Uhm...may I use your restroom?" Alex notices my mood change but doesn't force anything. He kisses the top of my head and helps me up. Once I'm stand, I feel the rush of the wine hit me and I begin to sway.

Alex grabs a hold of me and steadies me.

"Are you alright?" He asks concerned.

"I guess I did have a little too much wine. Do you mind getting me a glass of water?" I ask.

"Of course. Let me lead you to the restroom and I'll get us a couple of glasses of water."

Alex takes my hand and I wrap my arms under his and hold on tight as we head down the hall. I walk up to the restroom door and hold myself up with the door knob.

"Okay...I'll be out in a minute. Thank you."

Twenty-Five

I walk in the bathroom and lock it behind me. I lean against the door wishing I hadn't drunk so much. I sort of wish Alex would take me home so I can lie in my bed and pass out. Being with Alex feels too comfortable. His touch drives my skin wild and I'm afraid my drunken self might let things go too far. I'm also not ready to talk about home or my parents. Alcohol and sad stories don't mix.

I turn the faucet on and let the water wash over my arms and neck to cool me down. I just need to take it slow.

I use the restroom and wash my hands again and decide to just face whatever comes my way. When I turn off the faucet, I hear Alex talking with someone in the hallway, but I don't understand what they are saying. I open the door to see a perfect Abercrombie & Fitch specimen talking with Alex. Mr. Abercrombie's hair is so blond it almost looks white. It's in a high Pompadour fade that twirls at the top. His eyes look just like Alex's, bold blue sapphire jewels. He's just as tall as Alex and lean and chiseled.

They both look upset about something and look to be arguing, but in a language I don't understand.

When I take another step closer, they both turn to look at me.

I begin to inch forward and shyly smile at blondie and Alex.

"Hi." Is all I manage to say, with a small wave.

Alex's jaw tightens as if I interrupted something important and it makes me want to back away and apologize.

Alex turns to blondie, then me, with a calmer look.

"Mia. This is my brother. Lucius."

"Oh...very nice to meet you." I walk up and extend my hand.

Lucius looks to Alex then me and extends his hand.

"It's a pleasure Mia. I apologize for intruding on your...date, but I'm afraid my brother and I have urgent business to attend to."

Alex says something to Lucius in what sounds like old Latin, but I can't be sure. Whatever he said, sounded like it was a warning to Lucius.

"I apologize Mia. Something just came up and I'm afraid Lucius and I must take care of our current problem with urgency."

"Oh...I can totally catch a cab home. I don't want to interfere."

I feel as if Alex is trying to brush me off, so I begin to step back but then he grabs my hand and pulls me close to him.

"I've already called my private driver to take you home. He's waiting downstairs. Please know that I am truly sorry this came up. I wouldn't disrupt our evening if it wasn't urgent. I would like to see you again if that's alright?"

My hesitant look must have given me away.

Before I can answer, Alex tugs me into the living room. Once we are out of view of Lucius, Alex pulls me in closer and kisses me soft and deep. His arms explore my waist and then down to the top of my ass where he grips it. He pulls me in so close I can feel his erection. It shocks me but I'm turned on. My body heats and tingles all over, like I'm on fire. My legs begin to feel weak and just when I feel like I might lose my balance Alex pulls away.

"I've been wanting to do that all night. Actually, I've been wanting to do a lot more, but I know you want to take things slow."

I don't remember telling Alex I want to take things slow but I'm glad he knows. Though, at this moment, I could easily give into him and let him take anything he wanted, including my virginity.

Alex holds me by my waist, and I look up at him grateful for his patience.

"Thank you. I do want to take things slow. We still don't know much about one another. But no pressure. If this...whatever this is, doesn't work for you, it's okay. I know you are only here for a short while."

Alex runs his hands up and down my back and kisses my forehead.

"Actually, I think I will be here for quite some time. I won't be going anywhere any time soon. I would like to see where this goes if that's alright with you?"

Glad to hear that he is still interested, I smile and pull him in close, letting him wrap his arms around me tighter.

"Okay...let's see where this goes." I say with glee.

As I begin to pull away, Alex holds onto me and gives me a serious look.

"Mia...while we are seeing one another, I would like us to be exclusive."

Right then, my insides light up like fireworks. I was afraid Mr. Hottie isn't the one-woman sort of guy, but I'm surprised.

"Okay." Is all I manage to say with a big smile.

As Alex leads me out of his home, his brother Lucius gives us both a wary look. He doesn't seem to approve of me. I wonder what his deal is but decide I don't care right now.

As we walk down the sidewalk, Alex gives me a card with his cell number on it. I pull my phone out of my purse and dial his number and let it ring once before hanging up so he has my number.

When I look up, I see a blacked out Audi S8. The driver has his window down and is wearing a black suit. *Fantsy*.

Alex walks me to the car and opens the door for me. He leads me in and holds my face with both hands to gently kiss me. Afterwards, he gives the driver instructions.

"Please call me if you need anything. Once I have taken care of our urgent business, I would like to see you again."

I blush at the thought and shake my head yes.

We give each other one last longing goodbye look, and then he closes the car door and the driver takes off.

***

Saturday morning at Mocha's is almost as busy as a Friday night. It seems like everyone on campus is in the shop ordering. Thankfully I have both Mr. and Mrs. T. here to help me. I'm still learning the orders and it takes me a bit longer to fulfill. A little after an hour of my shift ending, I finally have a good pace down. I meant to leave at noon but hated leaving Mr. and Mrs. T. here on their own. I don't have to meet Sheriff Daniels for another 30 minutes anyway.

I finally decide it's time to go when things slow down. I go into the office and grab my bag and say my goodbyes before heading out. It's been a hectic morning and I'm already ready for sleep. Morning hours on the weekend are extremely early. I was clocked in at 6:00 a.m. this morning, in which I had to wake up at 5:00 to shower and get my day started.

I walk across campus and find my way to the campus quad. I find a bench and practically fall onto it I'm so tired.

As I begin to relax, the realization of seeing the Sheriff and hearing what he has found begins to wake me up. I wonder what has happened that the Sheriff would come all this way to talk to me. Whatever it is it must be really important.

"Mia?"

I look up and see the Sheriff heading my way. He is out of uniform and it's not a look I am use to. Sheriff Daniels is in his late fifties, with dirty blonde hair. He looks like he might have been a town catch back his younger days but is now an aged version of Kevin Costner.

"Hey Sheriff." I stand and give him a hug and then sit back down.

"Have a seat." I pat the open spot next me.

"So tell me...what's so important that you couldn't discuss it over the phone and had to come all this way to see me?"

"Well Mia...the whole thing is a bit difficult to explain. I'm afraid you will be quite upset with all of the events that have taken place. I guess...I should just start from the top." He sighs heavily.

"Please. Don't hold anything back. I want to know everything."

"Well... here it goes. First, sometime after you left, I finally received our forensic analysis back from Portland on everything we gathered at the crime scene. Turns out, there were actually two sets of boot prints on the property and the way the prints were aligned throughout the property indicates that there was a scuffle between the murderer and someone else. Basically, it seems like someone chased the murderer off."

"So someone out there knows who murdered my parents and tried to help but won't come forward? Why? If we have the evidence that they were only trying to help, why would they run off and just stay under the radar?"

I just don't understand. My parent's murderer is out there and so is a witness.

"I don't know Mia, but we are doing everything we can with the hope that someone will come forward. But that isn't everything." He says with a sigh.

"Please go on."

Twenty-Six

"A month ago, the station received an odd call. Someone was looking for information on the death of Isabelle and Dorian Blackbourne. Of course, our Officer didn't have any information on the mysterious Blackbourne duo, so no information was given. After a little more probing, the caller asked if there had been any murders in the area within the past few years and where to find information. That of course was a red flag for our Officer, so they began tracing the call. The Officer took the bait hoping that the other end of the line would hook as well so he gave a little information about the murder of your parents. The caller lasted on the phone long enough to get a good trace. The number ended up being a pay phone line in Great Britain near Cambridge University campus, where your parents worked. We didn't have much to go by, so we left it alone. But the inquiry made me suspicious, so I started digging back into the case. I went over and over the clues and nothing jumped out at me. I reviewed the notes again about the caller asking about the Blackbourne duo that were first given, so I looked them up in the FBI database.

The problem is, the names were blacklisted. No content available. Like whoever they are, they're being protected. Then, I looked up your parent's information in the system and it was like they didn't even exist. I did some more digging on their dates of birth, names, and date of deaths and I came across a news clipping on a couple who were killed in a car accident in Seattle, Washington in 1999. The only survivor of the crash was a two-year-old girl."

Sheriff Daniels pulls out a copy of the newspaper clipping with a picture of a man and woman I don't recognize holding a little girl. When I lock eyes with the girls' face, my entire body goes numb. I recognize the pale brunette with pigtails and freckles in a baby blue jacket because there is a picture just like this one in our family photo album. The little girl is me.

The article reads:

Thursday, October 22, 1999. A white sedan was driving east bound on the 405 when a black SUV slammed into the white sedan, pushing it into the left side guardrail. Upon the crash, the black SUV was seen speeding away from the scene of the crime. The accident was unfortunately fatal for the driver and passenger of the white sedan, leaving only one survivor in the rear seat. Wife Leah Williams and Husband Samuel Williams were killed instantly in the hit and run. Only survivor is their two-year-old daughter Mia Williams.

The Sheriff notices my shock and his suspicions are confirmed.

"I'm sorry to break this to you Mia. The man and woman who raised you are not who you think they are."

"This can't be right. I mean...my parents...they..." I can't seem to find the words.

"I contacted the FBI sometime after I found the article and reported my findings and suspicions. A couple of days later, two agents and a whole forensics team showed up at the station and gave orders that your parent's graves were to be dug up and their bodies transferred to their facility. The agents also had warrants to search your home and premises and take any necessary items. They ended up packing up all of your parents work...artifacts, books, etc., and took it with them. They also packed up document records and photos of you and the family. A week after everything happened, I called the agency wanting to get an update on the evidence and I was told that there is no record of any federal agents in Silverton, Oregon. That they never received a call from our station. No report, nothing. I searched for our crime files and the warrants that were left to us and they too were missing. Someone came in to the station and basically wiped everything clean, taking any and all evidence with them, even the bodies of your parents Mia."

Tears begin to pull around my eyes as I realize my parent's bodies are gone, and no one knows where they are.

I begin to cry hysterically.

The Sheriff reaches his arm around me to try and console me, but I can't help the overwhelming hurt.

"I don't understand. How did this happen? What the hell is really is going on?! Why would anyone want to take my parents bodies from their graves? Sheriff...they may not have been my birth parents, but they are my parents. They raised me. I don't care about anything else being taken, but their bodies? Why would someone do this?!"

I cry even harder. My eyes blur, my head begins to feel like it's going to explode from all the pressure and my body heats like I'm about to have another anxiety attack.

I try to calm down, but the body tremors take over and an unbearable heat rises in my body and I pass out.

When I awake, the Sheriff and Bianca are at my bedside. I look around and realize I'm in my dorm. I slowly sit up and think about crying again but I just can't.

My head is pounding like I drank a bottle of Vodka so I lie back down.

"Maybe you should take it easy Mia. You felt a bit feverish when I picked you up to bring you back to your dorm. Are you feeling ill sweetheart?" The Sheriff asks.

I roll over to my side and just stare out into the room. I want a cold shower because I do feel feverish but don't want to get up just yet.

"I'm fine." I say.

"I'm sorry that I had to tell you all of this, but I think you needed to know. There is something bigger happening here. I think you need to be extra careful. I don't know if anything that was taken leads to you, so I want you to take care of yourself. I want you know that I am doing everything I can to figure out who came to our town and turned things upside down. I won't give in until I have some answers Mia. But until then, I need you to be safe and most of all keep living your life. I know that's hard to ask, especially with everything that has happened, but you can't live in limbo darling. And you are right...they might not have been your birth parents, but they were good people. They did a fine job raising you." He pats my arm gently and rises from my bed.

My eyes water from his words. Yes, going on like everything is okay is going to be hard. There are so many unanswered questions. It's like my parents were living a double life. But they were good people. They loved and cared for me like I was their birth child. The love they had for me is unbreakable. I don't care who they were.

"Hey Sheriff...thank you. I know you are doing your best. You wouldn't have come all the way out here if you didn't care. I really appreciate everything you are doing."

I get up from the bed and hug him.

"Mia...you are like family. The Mrs. and I weren't able to have children, so we never had the opportunity to know what it's like to love a child deeply, as deeply as your parents loved you. I feel like I have some responsibility to you in their absence. I want you to call me if you ever need anything. You are like family. If you decide to ever come home, know that we would love to have you visit us." He says patting my back.

"Thank you...I will."

The Sheriff walks out the door and I suddenly feel alone again. I look up at Bianca and see her eyes filled my sadness. She sits by me and begins to stroke my hair as I lean my head on her shoulders. I'm so thankful I have her here with me. I don't know what I would do without her.

I wake up from a three-hour nap I decided to take after filling Bianca in on what the Sheriff told me. I was emotionally and physically drained and just needed time to reboot.

The minute I sit up, I decide I need a little light in my life, so I call Alex. The line goes straight to voicemail.

"Hey Alex...its Mia. Umm...if you don't have anything going on this evening, I would really like to see you. Call me."

I hang up the phone and immediately regret leaving him that message. I probably sound desperate. Oh well...what can I do.

Twenty-Seven

It's been three weeks since the Sheriff came to visit me and three weeks since I last spoke with Alex on our date. I couldn't sleep for the first couple of nights after the Sheriff told me what happened. I kept thinking about the man and woman I've known as my real parents as well as my biological parents.

The Leah and Samuel Williams I knew didn't have any family left. What if my biological parents have family?

I spent most of the first week searching the internet trying to find something that would give me any information about my biological parents, but I had little luck. I've tried not to allow the bad news from the Sheriff bring me into depression, so I've kept myself busy with school and work.

My personal life of late has felt so shitty that I don't really dwell on the fact that Alex hasn't called. He wouldn't want to get mixed up with someone who has so much drama anyway.

I knew Alex was out of my league from the get-go, so I try not to let it bother me. But every now and then, I think about him. I replay our evening in my mind and the feel of his touch. But then I come back to reality and feel like shit all over again.

Noah and I have since become really good friends. He now knows what very few know about me. It was hard keeping a smile on my face with such terrible news throughout the weeks. When I tried to lie about it he saw right through me. He didn't let it go until I confided in him. It was the best thing I ever did. He's been such a great shoulder to cry on when I need it.

Noah of course continues to pursue me. I think he does it mainly to make me laugh. Always telling me how much I want him. Noah knows that the date with Alex went well and the agreement Alex and I came to, but he also knows that Alex hasn't called.

I keep hoping Alex shows up out of nowhere or calls. I've tried calling him, but it goes straight to voicemail. I've only left one message, which was a couple of days ago, and still nothing. I've decided that if I don't hear from him by this weekend, I'm done chasing him. I might even give into Noah.

Noah and I get along so well and so easily. He's funny, charming and totally hot. Bianca has already asked if she can have her way with him but the thought of it drove me crazy, so I told her I have dibs. But I'm not sure why I said that because I still think about Alex.

Natalia even has a crush on Noah. She and I have been working the same shifts over the past couple of weeks and we've become absolute besties. It almost seems like we've known each other all our lives.

We finish each other's sentences and we are always thinking the same. We have so much fun working together that we forget we are working. We laugh so much that by the end of the day I feel like I've gotten the best ab work-out ever. She is like a sister I never had.

When Noah comes by Mocha's, which is at least every other day to visit with me, Natalia can't seem to form a complete sentence when he talks to her. It's actually pretty cute since he should be the intimidated one. She's drop-dead gorgeous.

Noah is great in so many ways but...I don't get that overwhelming heated feeling with him like I got with Alex. The chemistry Alex and I had is like no other.

Ugh...I know I have to be realistic. I'm not going to wait around forever. Tonight, it's over.

***

Friday nights at Mocha's is always packed. Luckily, Natalia is here to help me out.

"So...have you heard from this mysterious Alex yet?" Natalia asks.

"No...I've checked my phone a few times today and still nothing. I'm giving him until tonight to call me. If I don't hear from him, I think I am going to give into Noah." I sigh.

Natalia squeals with glee.

"I think you should just text Noah now. Why wait any longer?"

"I don't know. Something inside me just wants to wait. Alex has this invisible hold on me and I don't get why." I wine.

Natalia gives me a worried look.

"I hate to say this Mia, but it's been three weeks love. I think you should just forget about the guy."

"I just don't know if the chemistry is there with Noah. I like him a lot but not the way I like Alex. I also don't want to ruin a great friendship with Noah. He's so fun to be around and I would just die if I lost him as a friend if things didn't work out."

"Hey...how about this. We should all go dancing tomorrow night. Invite Noah and tell him there will be a group of us so it doesn't seem like a date. If things kick off between you and Noah...well, just see how it goes. At least there will be no promises or uncomfortable first date antics between you two."

"You know what, that actually sounds like a great idea. I love dancing and Bianca will totally be in. I'm sure she will bring along a group of guys and girls so we can even the odds. Okay...let's do it. If things heat up with Noah and I, we will just see how it goes. No promises. Easy."

Natalia and I jump up and down at the thought.

"I think it's time you move on from this Alex guy."

"Your right. I'm going to text Bianca the plan. Feel free to invite whoever you want. The more the merrier. Then I'll text Noah. Ooh...I'll tell him to invite friends as well. Maybe he will bring someone to temp you." I give her a shoulder roll.

"Oh yes please. If they look anything like Noah, I'm totally in." she says fanning herself.

I laugh at her and help her fan.

I text Bianca the plan and she immediately responds with excitement. I then text Noah the details and he replies with a smiley face and a thumbs up.

The rest of the evening winds down so fast and its already closing time.

Walking back to campus I look at my phone with utter disappointment. I was hoping my good energy and wishful thinking would somehow reach Alex and he would get the message to call me, but by the time I got to my room and dressed for bed, I gave up on that theory...and Alex.

Saturday morning I woke up feeling refreshed from a good night's sleep. Luckily, I have the day off from work so Bianca and I are going to get some laundry done and then go shopping for an outfit for tonight. I just hope she's not like Mandy when it comes to shopping. I want to get in and out of the mall as quickly as possible.

When we arrive back at the dorm from our shopping spree, we both plop down on our beds exhausted. We definitely bought more than we needed. I didn't bring many clothes from home with me, so I bought a few things here and there. Well maybe more than a few. Let's just say if Mandy were here, she would be pretty proud of me. We were at the mall for four hours and I ended up with six full shopping bags.

I miss Mandy all the time. I've talked to her at least four times since the Sheriff arrived. The first call was me unloading a ton of information about what the Sheriff told me. She was shocked and upset for me. She agreed with the Sheriff to not dwell on it all because what is done is done. Since my unloading, she calls me every couple of days to check up on me to make sure I'm still "living".

Lucky for her, I've never been the sort of person to allow depression consume me. I'm sort of like a rubber band, I bounce back pretty quick. It doesn't mean I completely shut out what bothers me. I just have the ability to push the thoughts and pain deep down until I have time for it.

"Okay...I'm going to take a long hot shower. I'm so beat. If I lie here any longer, I'm going to fall asleep." Bianca says while jumping off her bed.

"You do that. I'm going to lie here a bit longer. I'm so tired. I just need a little nap before tonight."

My eyes begin to get droopy and I catch Bianca take her shower caddy and leave the room.

Just as I'm about to drift off to sleep, my phone rings. I contemplate whether I want to answer it but think it might be the Sheriff or...even Alex.

I jump out of bed and dig in my purse for my phone. When I pull it up, I see a number I don't recognize.

"Hello?"

"Mia?" the man asks.

"Yes. Who is this?"

"It's Dr. Osborne. I'm sorry it took so long to reach you. I've been trying to find the right time to call you."

"Dr. Osborne? Why are you whispering?"

"To be safe."

"Safe from what? What's going on? Do you know anything about my parent's? My real parents?"

Dr. Osborne sighs.

"I can only imagine what you've been through. Your parents, the people who raised you were very good friends of mine. There is quite a bit of information I must tell you but not over the phone. I'm afraid what I will have to say will come as a shock to you."

"Well Doc. I think I've had enough shock to light a Christmas tree. I want to know everything. But I can't just hop on a plane to Great Britain. I have school and work."

"That's why I'm here on campus. Do you have time to meet now?"

"You're here?!"

"Yes. Mia, I don't have much time."

"Okay...okay. Where?"

Twenty-Eight

I meet Dr. Osborne in the library. I take the elevator down to basement level 2. It's quiet and I start to think this is a bad idea. The Sheriff did say stay safe and here I am meeting a man I don't know down in the basement of a Library.

Great way to start a horror story Mia!

But I don't care. I want to know what the hell is going on.

I walk down one of the main isles and find the Doc pacing back and forth.

"Dr. Osborne?"

"Mia."

Dr. Osborne looks to be the same age as my parents. Late fifties. A receding hair line and glasses that look to be ten years old. His suit looks to be just as old or older.

"I'm sorry to abruptly meet like this." The Doc looks nervous and agitated.

"Look Doc. Just be straight with me. What's going on? What do you know?"

"Let's have a seat shall we."

We walk over to the closest table and sit. The Doc looks around fearfully and fidgets in his seat.

"As you now know, your parents are not your real parents. The car crash that took your biological parents' life was no accident. It was intentional. They were after you. They wanted you dead."

"Who? Who wanted me dead?" I plead.

"Listen. There are things in this world you would never believe to be true. Your adoptive parents thought making a deal with the Council would protect you. It did...at least for a while. Your *Vis* just grew too powerful with age.

"What does *Vis* mean?

The Doc is talking so fast and incoherently I can barely keep up.

"Your parents were part of the Council but left when things got out of hand. The members were turning against the old ways. They've been watching you all your life. They've seen your Vis grow stronger with time. Your parents tried to conceal it as often as possible with the help of other allies by binding it dormant. Your parents were able to see that your emotions draw the Vis out and took every necessary precaution to ensure it remained dormant. In the end, the Council did not believe you could be contained. They know the others are after you. The others now want you for themselves. To use you against the Council. The Council is willing to go against the old ways to make sure the others don't get to you first, even if that means killing you. If you are taken by the others, the control the council has on them could be lost.

"What are you talking about Doc? You're losing me here. What Council and what others?" I nearly scream from irritation.

"Please remain calm Mia. The older you get, the spell binding your Vis dormant, weakens. The intensity of your emotions can draw it out. If that happens, if your Vis is brought out, everyone will be after you for your power. You have the ability to control it. But I must warn you, the Vis has light AND dark energy. All life is made up of equal light and dark, or good and evil. It is up to you which energy is brought about. The dark energy has taken the essence of

Saga's before you. You will have to learn how to harness the power and never let the dark energy outweigh the light."

"I don't understand any of this. Please just slow down and start from the beginning."

A noise from behind me makes us both jump. We turn and look but see nothing.

The Doc stands and there's true fear in his eyes.

"I've already risked too much. All you need to know is that your parents were good people who risked everything to protect you. They are coming for you Mia. All of them. But we've secured your protection. Old allies have come to help. They are bound to you and will do whatever it takes to protect you from the Council and the others, *the Cursed.*

The Cursed?

"I must go before they find out where I am. If they know I've been involved, they will..." The Doc falls silent.

"No...please don't leave. I need to know more." I begin to cry.

"There are still those who abide by the old ways and want to help. You will soon learn who they are. You will soon learn how important you are."

"Remain true to your good heart Mia. In times where you feel lost, remember who you are. Think about those who love and care for you. Never give in to dark thoughts."

Before I can get anything else out, the Doc rushes to the emergency stairs and leaves.

What the Fuck?!

I sit there letting the tears run down my face. I don't understand what is happening.

I'm so fed up with all of the mystery. I just want fucking answers.

I realize I'm starting to curse a lot more these days. My sadness has become anger. Anger at all the secrecy. At all of the unknown.

I dry my tears and decide no more. I'm going to eventually get to the bottom of all of this.

Back in my room I throw myself onto the bed and stare at the ceiling. I would usually curl into a ball and cry myself to sleep but for some reason I just can't seem to bring myself to do it. I've done enough crying. No more pity parties for me. The only thing I want to do right now is drown all this bullshit with alcohol.

Fuck it!

I jump out of bed and grab my shower caddy. I have two hours to get ready before we head downtown. When I open my wardrobe, I know exactly what I'm going to wear. My skin tight Red dress and black boots and I plan to top it off with red lips. I'm ready to drink and dance until everything spins and blurs.

***

We all meet in the parking lot of Mocha's. Bianca invited her friend Heather and Lily and a car load of guys. I join Natalia and her friend Veronica in her car as we wait for Noah to show. Noah pulls up in his truck with guys hanging out the windows, laughing and hollering.

Frat boys.

"Hey gorgeous! Wow. You look..."

"Lady in Red..." a frat boy sings out the back window.

I laugh and hear Noah telling them to shut up.

"You ready to go have some fun? Just try to keep your hands to yourself tonight. I know I'm irresistible, but we're going to be in a public place." Noah smiles.

I can't help but laugh at his smartass humor. I love it because it leaves a huge grin on my face.

"Yeah...yeah...I'll make sure to do that." I say shaking my head.

The bar is filled with people and the music playing loud. The ladies group together on the dance floor while the guys play pool, watching us like hawks. I overheard Noah's friend Jake say that the girls will end up getting them all in trouble before the nights over. Every time a guy would come up to us to dance, the glares Noah and the guys gave them could kill.

One guy walked up to me and wrapped his arms around my waist and Noah nearly lost it. Natalia and Veronica saw Noah coming and pulled the guy away before anything could happen.

Since Noah's friend Jake knows the bar owner, we were able to get drinks for half the price. We took shot after shot with the guys. I of course haven't done anything like this before, so I was feeling pretty buzzed way before anyone else.

A night of booze and dancing is exactly what I needed. I wanted it to black out the craziness in my life.

"I have to go pee. I'll be right back." I tell Natalia.

I push myself through the crowd and make my way to the back of the bar.

I see the restroom sign pointing down a long hallway. I make my way to the hall and lean against the long wall as I slowly walk. The drinks have really kicked in now.

When I get to the end of the hall, an exit door flies open. A tall muscular man stands there taking up the door frame. My vision is a little blurred by the alcohol and darkness of the hallway, so I squint to take a closer look.

I look up to see a 250 pound, 6'4 physique. I glide up his massively broad shoulders to a familiar face framed by a Mohawk with tattoos lined down the sides.

It takes a minute for my brain to register that I've seen him before. I point at him and begin to say something but then the creepy grin across his face makes my skin crawl.

As I begin to back up, fear paralyzes me when I see his eyes go pitch black.

Before I can turn to run, he grabs me, covers my mouth and pulls me out the exit door, dragging me away from the building and into a dark alley around the corner.

Twenty-Nine

I try to scream but my muffled cries are no match for the loud music playing in the bar.

He shoves my body up against the hard brick wall with my arms pinned to my side. His size and strength hold my 5'3, 130-pound frame with little effort.

The overbearing creep closes the distance between us, sniffing down my neck.

I want to scream but all I do is keep my head pinned to the side, trying to build some distance.

"What do you want from me?" I plead.

"Oh Mia. Marcus will be so pleased I finally have you. You are quite the specimen, and you smell so absolutely fucking delicious. I just want to taste you, all of you." He says with a growling hunger.

He leans his hard, heavy body into me. The heat that radiates from his large body is sweltering.

I squirm, feeling disgusted and smothered.

The fear of him holding me against my will seems to take over my body as it begins to tremor. I feel the anxiety attack coming.

Please not now. I tell myself.

He chuckles and pushes into me even more, allowing me to feel how much I arouse him.

Gross

"I never thought a Saga could get me so fucking hard. Surely Marcus won't mind if I try you out before I deliver you."

I whimper in disgust. This is not how I planned to lose my virginity. Raped by a steroid drug junkie.

I'm trembling even more and the heat inside me is building and rising.

If he weren't so disturbing, he may be considered sort of hot, but the way he looks at me with those black eyes, I feel like he wants to devour me like a cannibal.

It must be an effect from some sort of drug. Like acid or something.

"Don't you dare even think about it you fucking creep."

I spit at him and that of course sets him off.

He slams me against the wall again, making my body go limp. Pain surges in my head from the impact and the trembling gets worse.

Just as I'm about to try and scream I hear the bars exit door open.

"Mia? Are you out here?" Noah calls.

I stiffen with fear. Noah is just as tall as Creeper but he's not as stalky. For all I know Creeper might have a knife or a gun.

"Is that your boyfriend Mia?" Creeper whispers with venom.

"No. No...he's just a friend. Please don't hurt him."

Thankfully Noah doesn't see or hear us, and my silence gets him to go back inside the bar.

While distracted by Noah, I knee Creeper dead center in the groin. He grunts and let's go of me only for a second before slamming me against the wall again.

"Fight me all you want. You're too weak. You're power is dormant. That was their first mistake. Cry...scream...it will only give me more pleasure. I'm going to taste your blood and then I'm going to take what should be mine. I've been after you for nearly three years. I deserve a little taste."

"Please don't!" I plead.

He chuckles low and chilling. His aggressive lust repulses me. He snarls like an animal and I feel his breath on my neck. Whatever he is on is making him animalistic.

"Get off of me." I scream.

He thrusts against me once more, groaning to the sound of my plea. He begins to slowly reach down my leg with one hand while abusing one of my breasts with the other.

My eyes water from his assault, from the pain of his strong hands.

My body trembles again. I can feel it heat and boil from my anger and pain.

His laughter begins to fade and the pain of his hold drifts away. Suddenly I feel nothing. My vision blurs from my tears, then dwindles and all I see is black.

I feel as if I've left my body, like I'm lost in the dark. Within an instant, my vision reappears but all I see is red. My body awakens with fury, with absolute rage.

The anger I feel is dark and malevolent and consuming.

A scream wales from my mouth, and a florescent red light thrusts from my hands to the man pinning me against the wall.

The red light singes his skin and propels his body in the air and smashes it against a brick wall where he goes limp.

The red glow disappears and my body instantly falls to the floor. As the body tremors fade, I see a black dusty smoke leave my body.

I feel shattered and drained of energy.

I open my eyes and the malicious rage is now gone. I don't know what just happened to me. I felt lost while something else took over my body. I could only sense what was happening but had no control. All I know is that whatever just happened scared the shit out of me.

Trying to gain full consciousness, I hear Creeper get up and roar with anger.

I know I don't have enough fight in me.

My eyelids feel heavy, but I can sense he's coming for me.

Just when I think pain is going to have a new meaning, I hear his roar cut short.

I drag my eyes open to see a glimpse of a figure thrown down the alley.

I don't know how it happened but I'm happy by the thought of the creepers body striking the ground with such force it most likely killed him.

My strength is still weak, but I manage to prop myself on all four in order to stand. I look up and see a hand stretched out towards me.

"Are you alright Mia? Did he hurt you?" he says with concern and anger.

I can't believe it.

"Alex?"

Before I can lend Alex my hand, I'm terrified and shocked to see the deranged man standing only 10 feet away as if he wasn't just thrown against a wall.

Though his body looks burned, it also looks like his scorched skin is healing itself.

Alex turns to face him.

"Alexander. Your presence of late has been quite irritating. You've been keeping me from what's mine."

Mohawk guy looks at me and grins.

How the hell did he get up so fast? How is he not dead? How the fuck is he healing?

"Careful Brutus. I'm sure Marcus will be displeased with your be-havior." Alex says with anger.

Brutus is his name? Who the hell is Marcus? How do they know each other? What the shit?

Brutus hasn't moved his eyes away from me.

"You dare touch Mia...I will rip you to shreds. I nearly did once before, I will do it again."

Alex stands his ground in front of me and though I'm glad he's here, I'm afraid for him. I don't want him to get hurt. This Brutus guy is so much bigger than Alex.

"Alex...let's just go. There's something wrong with him. I think he's on drugs or something. Let's go and get help." I plea.

"Yes...Alexander. Why don't you run off like Mia suggests." Brutus begins to step forward.

"I will take your life Brutus without a second thought." Alex says calmly.

Alex's calm composure confuses me. He's not afraid of this Brutus guy and he should be.

"You will start a war. The pack will have your head." Brutus says.

"War has already begun."

I look behind me and see an opening to the street. Now's my chance to run.

Brutus watches me and knows exactly what I'm trying to do.

I get up and take off anyway and right before I can get to the end of the alley where I suddenly see Brutus, Lucius comes out of nowhere and strikes Brutus. He flies high into the air and then slams against a dumpster 100 yards away.

No...fucking...way...

Brutus jumps up faster than humanly possible and growls at Lucius.

"Well if isn't big bad Brutus. I thought I smelled Dog." Lucius teases.

The moment Brutus sets eyes on Lucius, they widen and darken with fury. Fangs protrude from his mouth and claws begin to grow from his hands.

I edge up against the wall, shaking my head in disbelief.

Brutus is now half man, half...monster.

I look to Alex and Lucius wondering if they see what I see. Fearing what might become of us.

They stiffen in a defensive stance and then draw silver blades from their back. Their eyes begin to aluminate so blue that they almost turn white.

This can't be happening.

"Now Brutus...is that any way to treat an old friend?" Lucius mocks as he paces.

"Filthy fucking leeches. The pack has already claimed the girl. Hand her over or you both die." Brutus growls.

Lucius chuckles.

"Careful Belletore. You know I have a bit of a temper. You may see your brother Darius in the afterlife sooner that you hoped." Lucius threatens.

Brutus snarls with rage and then lunges at Lucius, but Lucius runs up the brick wall and summersaults backwards over Brutus. Lucius lands a blow to Brutus' back, slicing him so deep blood gushes.

Brutus roars and turns to Lucius slashing over and over but missing Lucius each time. Lucius is too fast.

Brutus snarls, then turns looking for me. When he sets his eyes on me, he lunges towards me.

I back up, eyes wide with fear.

Alex steps in front of me and grabs Brutus by the throat and throws him back towards Lucius as if he was a bag of potatoes.

Alex and Lucius circle Brutus with their weapons in hand, like they are Lions closing in on their prey.

"This isn't over. I will have Mia one way or another. Her power is no longer dormant, and Marcus will soon hear of it, as well as the *others*. You can't protect her from us all."

Brutus snarls, bends to one knee, then leaps high over the building and vanishes.

Alex and Lucius both turn to one another with worry and then face me.

Thirty

I'm up against the wall panting from fear and anxiety of what just happened. I'm breathing so fast and hard I think I'm about to pass out.

I look at Alex and see that his eyes have gone back to their normal sapphire color and he looks at me solemnly. His weapon has been put away and he no longer looks like the hunter after his prey.

My eyes burn with hot angry tears for my life has just been spun around and fucked over twice more. I feel like I've just risen from a puddle of mud. Everything is murky.

I should be scared of Alex and Lucius but I'm not. I'm just angry as hell.

"What the fuck is going on?"

"Mia..." Alex reaches for me but I shake my head no.

"Don't fucking touch me Alex. I want to know what the fuck is going on and who the fuck you guys are."

"Well...your up brother. She's all yours." Lucius says with sarcasm.

"If you'll let me explain..." Alex says.

Before Alex can say anything, I hear Natalia calling me. She comes running around the corner and when she sees Alex and Lucius her eyes go wide. She looks at me and then to them.

"What are you doing here?" Natalia asks Alex.

I look at her and then at Alex in confusion.

"Wait...you know him?" I ask credulously.

"She was attacked by Brutus. We almost didn't get here in time." Alex says.

"I thought he was summoned back by his pack. Why was he here?" Natalia asks.

"He shouldn't be." Alex says.

I stand there shocked by the exchange. I don't even know what to say.

"Well brother. I told you my theory. I think Brutus fancies Mia. He has been after her for quite some time. I believe the Brute has become obsessed with your dear Saga darling." Lucius says nonchalantly.

"Okay...I keep hearing this word. What the hell is a Saga?"

"If Brutus is ignoring his packs orders, he is a loose cannon. You two should be watching Mia more carefully. From a distance... Alex. You've already gotten yourself too involved." Natalia says as she begins to twirl ideas in her head.

"We wouldn't have to babysit her if you would do your job. Why has she not been changed?" Lucius asks Natalia.

Changed?

Natalia looks to me and I see sorrow in her eyes.

"Okay...that's enough from all of you. I need one of you to explain what the fuck is going on?" I say angrily.

"You certainly have quite the mouth on you." Lucius says smiling.

Alex swats Lucius in the ribs.

"Mia...there is a lot to explain and I'm afraid you aren't ready to hear it all just yet. I think we all need to sit and talk about this." Natalia says.

Before I can contest, I hear Noah and Bianca calling me and Natalia's name. They both round the corner and halt at the sight of us all, knowing they might have interrupted something. Bianca smiles at me and Alex but Noah looks pissed.

"Sorry to interrupt guys but we've been looking for you Mia. I see now why you've disappeared. Nice to see you again Alex." Bianca says with a glowing smile.

The moment Noah hears Alex's name, his jaw tightens and his fists form.

"We've been looking for you Mia. I...we were worried. You should have told us you were with...him." Noah says.

Alex looks at Noah with a raised eyebrow and then strides closer to me.

"My apologies. I asked Mia to meet me out here so we could talk. I wanted to personally apologize for not being able to return her calls." Alex says as he pulls me close to wrap his arm around my waist.

I look up at him with a "fuck you" look and shove his arm off.

"So...why didn't you answer her calls?" Bianca asks so boldly.

"Bianca!" I scold.

"I was out of the country for an urgent business matter and I was unfortunately in a location with no reception. Land lines aren't common in the middle east." Alex says.

"Oh wow. And here I thought you were blowing my bestie off. Glad you had good reason. I would hate to have to kick you in the balls." Bianca says.

"Bianca!" I yell again.

She looks at me and shrugs her shoulders.

"I'm also glad you didn't have to do that." Alex says with a smirk.

Okay...this is all too weird. Noah and Alex are having a pissing match with their glares and stances. Natalia looks at me nervously and sorrowful, Bianca keeps giving Lucius her "let's fuck" eyes with Lucius totally digging it and giving Bianca his "I'm sexy and totally down" look. I don't have time for all of this bullshit.

"Well guys. It's getting late and I'm ready to hit the sack. Super tired and all."

"I can take you home." Both Noah and Alex chime in.

"Uhm...actually I am going to ride home with Natalia. I need to talk to her about our schedules for next week to see if she can switch with me one night. Bianca? Do you mind taking Veronica home?"

Bianca snaps out of her eye fucking contest with Lucius.

"Oh sure. How about you? Do you need a ride?" Bianca asks Lucius.

Oh my God...there was double meaning in that question.

"I actually have some business to tend to with my brother here." Lucius says.

"Brothers? Nice." Bianca says flashing her sexy smirk.

"Some other time...? Lucius leans forward wanting a name.

"Bianca...and yours is?" She asks.

"Lucius. Very nice to meet you Bianca."

The steaminess between them right now is even getting me worked up.

"Okay then...well time to go." I shove Bianca forward while dragging Natalia with my free hand.

When Natalia and I get in the car, I unload.

"What the fuck is going on? How do you know Alex and his brother? Who is Marcus? What is a pack? What the fuck is a Saga? And who or what the fuck is Brutus?"

"Calm down Mia. Let me find a place to pull over. I'm sure Alex and Lucius are right behind us so we can all talk."

I turn around and I don't see any cars behind us.

"I don't see another car behind us."

She half smiles at me and pulls over at a nearby park.

We get out and walk to a picnic table. I sit down while Natalia paces back and forth. Before I get frustrated from her stalling, Alex and Lucius appear behind her.

What the?

I look at the parking lot and I don't see a car next to Natalia's. I look around for another car but find nothing.

"Where did you guys come from?"

Lucius gives me a devilish smile and winks at me as he sits on the edge of the table across from me.

Alex stands next to Lucius and looks at me solemnly.

"Alright Mia. This is going to be a lot to take in so please bear with us." Natalia pleads.

"A moment please. Before we begin. Brutus said that Mia's powers are no longer dormant. We must all take precaution if this is true." Lucius tells Natalia and Alex.

Alex looks to Natalia and then Lucius.

"That can't be. I haven't performed the ceremony yet. Her powers can only be released once I perform the spell."

I listen to them continue to talk about me as if I'm not there and anger begins to build in me. I stand up feeling an intense heat filling me up. The trembling begins again, and my impatience turns to rage. Before I can calm myself down, I start to see a red glow emanating from my hands.

"This is not good." Lucius says.

"Mia...breathe. You must calm yourself." I hear Alex say.

But my vision begins to fade, and I find myself in the dark again. Like I've left my body. I can hear Alex and Natalia speaking to me, but I can't figure out where they are.

Suddenly, a gust of air rushes past me.

When I open my eyes, I'm on the ground looking up at the sky. When I rise to sit up, it looks as if the picnic table and grass around me has been burned. That same black dusty smoke pours out from my body and I feel drained again.

I look around and call out to Natalia and Alex. Alex reappears and slowly closes in on me. He comes down to the ground to hold me and caress my hair.

"What just happened? Where are the others?" I ask confused.

"They are safe. Mia...there is much to explain but we must take it slow. Please try and remain calm. We don't want to activate your Vis. You are not yet able to control it."

Alex helps me up and I feel so dizzy. I feel like I could pass out.

"My what? Vis?" I ask, barely able to remain awake.

"I think we should get you somewhere safe. I promise, I will tell you everything you want to know."